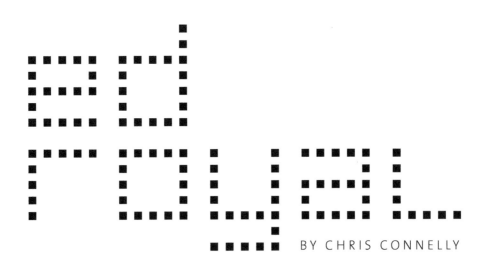

BY CHRIS CONNELLY

SHIPWRECKED INDUSTRIES

ISBN-13: 978-0-9664065-1-1
ISBN-10: 0-9664065-1-6
Library of Congress Control Number: 2010909026

Published by Shipwrecked Industries
July 2010
FIRST EDITION

ed ruscha

1 · THE GRASS LOOKS GREY

The grass looks grey. If you look away from the road, it could be a huge jungle. If you hold your hand up and block out the telegraph pole, it's somewhere else in the world and you are giant. The grass looks grey, like a black and white photograph of the grass, and there is nobody else here, the bus has long gone, away down the windy road. No sounds now, except for the mental bees in the bushes. You stop to open your bag and pull out the tranny radio. New batteries. "Heaven on the Seventh Floor" by Paul Nicholas on Radio One. Don't like that one, but leave it on to cover up the mental bees, they sound a bit too mad, like they might attack, because it's going to rain, and they'll all drown, got to hurt something before you die, got to use up that sting before you die.

The field with the caravan, nothing in the field, open the gate, nothing to escape, no cows or sheep. Dirty white caravan with the filthy green Morris Minor beside it. Walk across the field, the Radio One afternoon DJ and his posh voice reading out requests.

Caravan looks like it could be a space shuttle against the grey sky turning black, first drops of rain, wonderful Radio One, first droplets of rain, "Would you play a song for my mum," the posh English DJ, "This is for all mums everywhere..."

"Dad, it's me..."

2 · TWO PEOPLE IN A ROOM

The room is cold. There is a fireplace, but it is empty, a gaping black slack-jawed mouth staring. There are several large cardboard boxes piled up in the middle of the floor, and several suitcases too. It is a large room, a sewing room? A drawing room? Ornate white cornicing and two very large windows that allow a view of bare trees and a wintry garden outside, flanked by the skeletons of bushes like so many thin, bony, grasping hands coming from the hard soil.

By the door in the room is a girl, maybe thirteen or fourteen, and by the window is a girl, maybe thirteen or fourteen. One has long dark hair, one red. The girl by the window is wearing a green school uniform, green skirt and blazer, white shirt and tie loosened around the collar; the girl by the door, the red-haired one, has jeans on and a bright red sweater. They stand in silence. They do not look at each other.

A woman's voice is heard elsewhere in the house, shouting. Three syllables only, rapidly together, but the words are indecipherable: "TAH TAH TAH!" The emphasis on the last syllable, "Tah tah TAH," the end of the last one tailing off quickly but with a note of despair underneath the anger, followed by a man's retort, his two syllable retort, "HA HIR," the emphasis, again on the last syllable, "Ha HIR!" Then a pause. Then the sound of a big door closing–not slamming–but when it closes, it makes a heavy rattle, an expensive, self-satisfied rattle. Then a pause.

The girls continue to stare, not at each other. The one by the window is not even looking out the window; the one by the door has white, tight lips, shown up by the crimson of her sweater. Her anger is obvious, it is too large and she is too young to have control over it. The girl by the window carries an equal weight in sadness.

"This is because of you," spits the red sweater, a theatrical whisper.

"No, no it's not, it's because Mum and Dad don't like each other and keep quarrelling," says the uniform, her voice small and resigned.

"Yes, and that's still your fault, it's still your fucking fault," red sweater no longer whispering, but shouting.

"Why?"

"Why?" mimics red sweater, "Why, why, why, why, why, why, why, WHY?"

She picks up a thick glass ashtray from on top of one of the boxes and throws it hard at the girl in the uniform.

It connects fleetingly with the side of her head, but continues through the window, smashing the pane entirely. The girl in the uniform shrieks quickly and brings her hand to her head. There is a little patch of blood. The cold air sweeps in from outside, and the girl in the red sweater opens the door and leaves the room, slamming it hard.

Silence.

3 · LIFE IN A DAY

That summer painted its story cryptically and subliminally, revealing itself at first in subtle stages, far too subtle for my impatient sensibilities. I was officially free from the constraints of school forever. I say "officially" because I had hardly paid heed or lip service to any matters scholastic for a good couple of years. But now–no more the charade of rising every morning and donning the uncomfortable blue uniform, the grey or white shirt, the regulation tie, and charcoal trousers.

The airwaves were vibrant with the propulsions of the fast, beat-laden chart music of the time, all volcanic drums and space. The streets of my city seemed bright and flecked with an indelible optimism as I flitted from club to club at night, home to job during the day, all strung together with a complex web of joints, drink, and anything else that was available as I built myself thousands of destinies on an hourly basis. It wasn't just me, of course–probably everyone my age felt that way that summer; we had not entered the real world of strikes, Thatcher, and chronic unemployment. There was a bright sheen to everything; blousy, billowy clothing, impossible haircuts, and armies of accessories dolled up the dance floors.

That summer was the last supper with childhood, before buckling down to careers or further education. Of course, I was buckling down to neither of these things, as will become apparent. I had not the remotest idea what was in store for me, and I had no plans or ambitions stretching beyond the upkeep of my self-sufficiency as a bon vivant.

That summer, when I cast my mind back to it (which is all I do), all I see is one bright, illuminated frame, like one of these giant ones in the National Gallery, a frame of euphoric freedom that tasted of pernod and blackcurrant, scented by John Player Special, hashish, and roses, with a soundtrack of excited chatter and laughter.

Turn that frame over and it's as dense and toxic as lead, uniform grey, and dead silent, its smooth surface destroyed by vicious scratches.

That summer turned very quickly into a dark palindrome, a black matching mirror held up against it. You'll see.

Nothing felt like goodbye, of course, nothing does at that age. That time was no time, the early summer in the wake of school's conclusion punctuated by celebratory parties at clubs and affluent domiciles the length and breadth of the city. The parties did not feel at all like farewells as much as statements of status and intent.

Fresh out of uniform, classmates would show up at clubs such as Annabel's and Buster Brown's in actual cars, wearing suits, watches, and cologne—at eighteen, looking like their fat, golf-playing fathers. The girls plastered in the not-so-long-ago-forbidden makeup, hair in the confusing and asymmetrical styles of the time.

One night at Annabel's, a known adversary of mine from school, Hamish Grey, a textbook rugby-playing bully, got thrown out late in the night, drunkenly masturbating on the dance floor whilst "Young Guns (Go For It)" blared out of the speakers. It was almost poetic because it was as if he had finally bared his soul and shown himself to us for what he was: a red-faced, ugly, weak bully.

I was not inclined towards these people at all. I was not riding in the fast lane, but I was definitely along for the ride, and had been for a few years now. The going out, the going out every night. Staying at home was like sitting on a grave in poor company, staying at home was beyond toxic and I won't talk about it just now.

Oh, those nights! Spilling onto Lothian Road, or the High Street, the sky still with that sedate glow although it was 1 am or later. The height of a Scottish summer, laughing, screaming, and singing into the night's concession to the dawn, dawn's concession to the night. The acrid taste of your last John Player Special in suicidal harmony with the taste of the alcohol in your mouth. Maybe a long kiss with the girl you walked out with, pressed into a Georgian doorway, your friends, walking away, roaring and laughing, "C'mon tae fuck youse two!"

More tongues and breathy nervousness in the back of a black ambulance, pulling up silently outside a house in the nether reaches of the city. "Try no tae make any noise, if ma mum wakes up she'll go fuckin' spare," whispered giggling as you are led upstairs.

Those nights, shapeless procession up the North Bridge, past bands of jeering neds, past the violated ruins of kebabs and baked potatoes, joined by disparate rivers and lakes of piss and vomit. Cops slowing down to stare, your heart speeding up, the acid overtaking the booze, polarizing the red-faced masks of the "see you jimmys." The hard wide mouths and their "I'm gonnae fuckin' pagger you, ya cunt" against the white/grey cold flesh of the cops, staring for a reason to do you in.

These nights, streaked mirror on granite relief,
Black ambulances in a row outside,
Smoke-stroboscope night,
Haunts, growling on gravel,
Sucking people off the paved lightning,
Of the dance floors and bars,
Whether you want to or not,
It is time to go home.

4 · NIGHTCLUBBING

"There's a wee one skinner in the back, big man. Beside the orwack, it's under a folded-up rubber glove." Ali walked by the checkout where I was stationed. We both worked at a large supermarket and we both relay-raced joints with each other, hiding them in the back and letting the other one know where it was hidden. This was what we had been doing for about two years, since we started work here You had to do something to take your mind off the ennui of selling groceries to the populous of much of the south of Edinburgh.

Ali was working out on the floor today, slapping price stickers on boxes of styling mousse and shampoo. My break was in ten minutes. It probably seemed strange that I would want to go into the back of the store on my break–there was a perfectly serviceable and dismal break room upstairs–but the management liked me, and I think as long as I did my job impeccably (which I did) they left me alone.

Ali and I had started on the same day, back a couple of summers ago when the supermarket had opened to considerable fanfare in the neighbourhood, putting to shame the Co-ops and Tescos and Spars, sad relics of shopping in the seventies. We had both attended the same "orientation" interview, which had us in stitches, and we became firm friends after that. We both worked two evenings during the week after school and Saturdays. We didn't attend the same school, but shared similar tastes in music, girls, drink, drugs, and making fun of the ludicrous uniforms we were made to wear at work. It meant I always had money in my pocket which granted me an exquisite freedom, allowing me to dismiss my home life and come and go as I pleased. This horrified my mother, who was adamant that I contribute to household expenses, but to her protests, as usual, I paid no heed.

I sat in the back smoking the joint with a cigarette burning to cover up the hash smell. Not that this was a problem as the back had an overpowering pungency, its bouquet a mixture of everything from pine floor cleaner and bleach, to wine, to every foodstuff imaginable. For this is where all the broken bottles and packets came and they were thrown into the mass grave of the orwack machine. It was a giant canister with a lid and a lock that compacted all of the damaged goods into one manageable lump, although I never saw what happened to the manageable lump after it was removed. "Aye, they probably feed it tae cows or gie it tae the orphanage," Ali cackled in a stoned frenzy one afternoon.

That evening, I was going to a party—another of the when-will-we-see-each-other-again-let's-keep-in-touch pointless affairs—but this time hosted by my ex-girlfriend, the beautiful Jackie Munro. I had been with her all the way through the fallout of her parents' divorce which, although she had never talked much about it with me, had taken its toll on her. She had chosen to live with her father in a huge house far too big for the two sullen occupants. I gathered her mother had remarried quickly, but everything else was talked about in vague half-finished sentences. Jackie lived very near me and my home life, which I, too, was hesitant to talk about.

Her father's lengthy absences due to work meant that we spent a lot of time at her house and a lot of that time in her bed, with little need for conversation; although sometimes after sex she'd open up a little, speaking in a hushed Miss Jean Brodie voice, enunciating and accentuating like a 1940s' school textbook. It was quite a turn on, alongside her slightly goth-goes-to-boarding-school look and her love of Siouxsie and the Banshees and Simple Minds.

We didn't ever officially split up. We just needed each other for a while and then we didn't need each other, that's all. We both went to the same school and were in the same year so it was just as well our unofficial "breakup" was not an acrimonious one like my parents' or hers.

We were both at George Heriot's, a fearsome, gothic-looking antiquity perched across the street from the Royal Infirmary Hospital and beside Edinburgh College of Art. When I first started going to Heriot's, there were no girls; it was an all-boys school: short trousers, blazers, and caps, running up and down treacherous unlit spiral staircases, trying to avoid the pupil hierarchy of bullies and rugby. When I first started going to Heriot's, it was 1974 going on 1820. Such were the terrifying teachers in flowing black gowns, staring with considerable ill-temper at the class staring back in terror. When the gates opened to females a few years later, it was like throwing a group of bewildered gazelles into a cage full of polar bears. The boys were at once delighted and sorely betrayed, mystified and cowardly. The girls were at once bold and mousy, studious and bawdy.

Somehow Jackie and I got talking to each other. I liked her a lot but considered her completely impossible, from a distant world where boyfriends were nineteen and no longer in school, and sat stubble-faced outside the school gates to pick up their fare at 3:15 every day.

As soon as I found out that Jackie did not have a boyfriend, I asked her to come with me to the Odeon to see the Specials. I had bought two tickets, three pounds each, and between buying them on a Friday afternoon after school, and approaching her with the idea on Monday morning, I spent the entire time inventing scenarios that ranged from her yielding bliss (Friday night) to her blushing and walking away (Saturday morning) to her snorting and saying "No" incredulously (Sunday morning) to her laughing and telling me to get lost (early Monday morning). So, when I plucked up the nerve and approached her on the way in to morning assembly and she said "Yes, that'd be great!" my heart exploded.

"Want to go to a party after work, Ali?" I asked him as he pushed bottles of revitalizing conditioner onto a shelf. "It'll be really shite."

"Aye, okay, why not?" he said.

"Good, it's Jackie's. There'll be a load of snobs and rugby lads from my school, we can get pissed and take the piss out of them."

"All right big man, quick pint doon the way first, aye? Maybe a wee smoke?"

"Right you are."

"Doon the way" was either the Canny Man's pub or the Merlin Roadhouse, the latter being a real dump erected in 1970 or thereabouts for god knows what reason. It reminded me of the Crossroads Motel, perhaps they were cashing in on the phenomenal runaway success of the television soap opera of the same name. However, it was within spitting distance of work and not as "nobby" as the more upper class Canny Man's. I'd take the Canny Man's any day: most of the staff disagreed with me and did a lot of their drinking, fighting, and probably sleeping at the Merlin.

Admittedly, the Merlin Roadhouse could be a lot of fun if you were stoned, watching the people you had worked with all day trying to pick each other up or throwing punches during arguments punctuated by vomiting and laughter. Otherwise, the place was a pit.

So a quick pint at the Merlin it was. A very quick one, as our co-worker Colin "Rambo" Ramsey—a stuttering, doughy thug from the meat department, all rolling flesh and barely-formed facial hair under a white, blood-stained trilby (required uniform)—happened to be parked at the bar. He had been, apparently, since his shift ended at about half past two that afternoon. It was now half past eight, actually more like quarter to nine, and here he was, probably about twenty-four pints in, by my calculation. It sounds incredible, but it was unlikely that he took a break. He just didn't have that kind of talent. He found something (drinking, for example) and doggedly went at it until he either passed out or got beaten up or just got thrown out. I wondered which it would be tonight.

Ali and I had entered the darkened bar, instantly recognizing Ramsey's stuttering roar. He immediately saw us and it was almost touching to see his face light up at the sight of such familiar adversaries. Colin hated our guts and had made this plain on the day we started. He paused while (perhaps) changing "insult" gears. "Are youse two poofs gonnae suck each other off then, ya cunt?" he inquired. "'Cos ye'd b-b-b-better dae it the noo, 'cos ye willnae be able tae efter I've fuckin' b-b-b-battered the two o' yez."

We ignored him, of course, and ordered our lagers. After about thirty seconds the drone of his voice blended in with the blip-blip-blip of the Space Invaders machine in the corner, which was also being ignored.

We drank up and left him to it. By that time a few others from work had drifted in to entertain him. Ali and I nipped down a quiet lane to smoke a joint. Ali, ever the historian, told me that someone from his school had been raped in this very lane, "By someone wearin' Bay City Rollers trousers, fuck's sake!"

We walked back to the main road and decided to walk to the party. It was a brilliant evening and we were both nicely stoned, the lager providing a cushion. At Bruntsfield we detoured from the main road and crossed The Links and then The Meadows, two parks separated by one road. We stopped at a playground to skin up and smoke another joint while sitting on the swings, rocking back and forth idly. Our giggling conversation recalled a story overheard in the work canteen about "Rambo" Ramsey's mother making soup out of pigeons he shot from the roof of the family house in Oxgangs. "Fuckin' shootin' pigeons oaf a roof fur 'is tea!" Ali screamed and coughed at the same time, hysterical. "His fuckin' ma's as fuckin' stupit as he is!"

Eventually we ended up outside Annabel's discotheque, paranoid, as the two bouncers stationed outside the door leered at us. I pulled the creased invitation out of my back pocket. We were still dressed from work: grey trousers and white shirts. At least we had removed our elasticated (regulation) bow ties and name badges; we would have to do like this.

"Ties the night, lads," monotoned the huge bouncer on my right.

"Aye, but it's my girlfriend's party. She doesn't care," I monotoned back.

"Ties the night, lads," he monotoned again.

Just then, Hamish Grey walked up with two of his rugby cronies, dressed up and drenched in Hai Karate or Blue Stratos aftershave lotion.

"Look who it isnae!" he boomed, sneering. There were too many teeth in his tiny mouth.

"Hamish, man, I heard you were in the hospital," I said, concerned.

"What are you fuckin' talking about?"

"Aye, I heard it was wanker's cramp."

"I'll see you later, pal," he said, the sneer becoming more toothy. "After I seen Jackie in the bogs, that is!"

He and his cronies cruised in, laughing. The bouncers stared past us as Ali and I pulled out our work-uniform bow ties and snapped them into place. "Ties the night, lads," I monotoned and we walked in.

Inside the same old affluent young Scotland was whiling away time dancing, drinking, and, above all, talking. Ali and I stuck out horribly in our creased and lived-in work clothes. We had removed the bow ties and Ali gleefully started mocking everyone loudly. "You simply MAHST CAHM riding with us this weekend! Oh do say yes!" I ordered pints. The music was too loud for Ali to be heard by anyone except me.

"Well, I'd join you old chap, but the bally wange wover's on the blink again!" I replied in my mock upper-class accent.

"Hello, Adam." I turned and saw Jackie. She looked amazing in a black cocktail dress with short sleeves and a low-dipped neck, her black hair shiny, wearing her signature black eyeliner. She was also wearing a particularly subtle perfume. I wondered if we could start going out again that night.

"You look amazing."

"Thanks," she smiled. "Hi, Ali."

"All right, Jackie!" Ali winked.

"I really hope you pair aren't going to stand here at the bar all night and make fun of my guests." Her liquid gold voice was cool and warm at the same time.

She smiled conspiratorially. It was a short smile, she seldom smiled but when she did, it could be like someone kicking the back of your knees, making them buckle.

"I'm just here to pickpocket, baby, I don't want any bother." I smiled back.

"Well, isn't it a shame I don't have any pockets!" she winked and turned away. "Don't leave without dancing, boys!"

"God, fuckin' hell, Ali!" I said, shaking my head and taking a gulp of my pint.

"I know, big man, I know, but she's away tae Aberdeen, is she not?"

"Yep, in September, Aberdeen Uni."

We stood at the bar and talked about our loose plans to get a flat together, that we wouldn't be able to afford it with just the two of us, that we needed a couple of other people. I had always had this dream of having a flat in the New Town, some huge Georgian place on Great King Street or somewhere, waking up in a huge room with high ceilings, but we would probably end up near Leith or maybe Marchmont. Ali lived with his parents in a tiny house in Oxgangs. His sister had moved out already and had a flat in Tollcross, which she shared with two girlfriends. She worked at a hairdresser's and let us crash in her living room whenever we wanted after a drunken night downtown.

I lived in Morningside, very near where we both worked and very near where Jackie lived. My mother had thrown my father out in about 1972, claiming that he had been sleeping with his secretary. I didn't know what that meant and no one was about to explain it to me. I came home from school one day and she had almost finished painting the kitchen blood red. Every wall, shiny blood red. It smelled like oil paint, a thick, heavy, choking smell. My father didn't come home that night and my mother and I ate a dimly-lit dinner of fish cakes and tinned spaghetti in a terrible silence. I saw my father only occasionally after that. Eventually he died, but I prefer to think that I just stopped visiting. The visits were as arduous as my home life. Both my parents were very highly strung and I probably was as well. My mother grew up near Coventry, when the place had been bombed in the Second World War. Any noise shook her to the core and she seemed to compensate by screaming as much as she could against the offending noise. My childhood years were spent in peril trying to play as quietly as I could. Long, tense silences interrupted by a sudden sound and shrieking. Then sobbing. Then silence again.

As soon as I was old enough to go out and play, I'd spend entire days in the park or at school friends' houses or just walking the streets of Edinburgh. I became an expert on the bus routes and times and would often take buses to the outer reaches of the city, exploring silently humming industrial estates and deserted suburbs for no real reason except to stay out of the house. The arguments started when I was about thirteen, right after Dad died. I can't remember how or why they started, really, I can't. They just sort of grew organically out of our lives. Things, of course, had not been right since Dad had gone and when he died I did feel on my own. Perhaps it was a battle of wills, but our life was so quiet, so impenetrably thick with silence. How did these incredible sounds just grow out of nothing? Out of the afternoon? My walks became longer and I would jump at the chance to spend the night at friends' houses until my mother became this peripheral figure in my life. A coiled snake that only once in a while would come out. Sometimes in an act of motherly kindness; usually in a fit of anger.

I remember coming home from school one day to see that she had painted *Is there a home for battered mothers?* in black on my bedroom wall and torn down all my posters. It was right around the time I had started seeing Jackie and I am sure that had something to do with it. I had made the mistake of bringing Jackie home after school one day, the first and last time. I had left her in my room to go and make coffee, and my mother had whispered angrily through clenched teeth to "get that stupid bitch out of my house, you've got homework to do" and promptly thrust a bowl of peapods into my hands. "Shell them," she said, and left the room...

The night wore on and Ali and I got drunk, made more fun of Scotland's future, and danced. We both danced with Jackie, my fists stabbing the air while Spandau Ballet's "I Don't Need This Pressure On" pumped through the club. Ali danced with her to the chirpy, inane sound of Haircut 100 doing "Love Plus One." I was glad it wasn't a smoocher.

We said our goodbyes late. Jackie looked the happiest I had ever seen her. She embraced me and I whispered in her ear that I thought we should spend the night together.

"Go home you drunkard," she whispered back playfully and Ali and I walked off into the night singing the "ay ay ay ay ay" refrain to "Love Plus One."

5 ▪ I PROMISED YOU A MIRACLE

The living room was illuminated by a solitary bedside lamp situated on a small end table at the end of a sofa. A soft yellow light barely illuminated the occupants, of whom there were five, including myself.

I was at Ricey's bit. Ricey Rankine, otherwise known as Rolls Royce, or just plain Roller, was a bad boy from Edinburgh Academy. Another rich kid gone wrong, who'd decided selling and taking drugs was far more agreeable than following in his dad's footsteps to high finance the honest way.

I knew Ricey from his hanging around the same circle of Heriot's druggies: he was a bit of a legend in that respect. He'd done smack, I'd heard. Like most rich kids, he tried to speak as if he'd grown up in the schemes but he couldn't quite carry it off and every so often his pampered, moneyed accent would peep through. His money and access to the best drugs forgave him this, however.

His flat was not a frequent haunt of mine. I tended to stick to Colin's in Morningside for my hash, but I was welcome enough at his Montgomery Street pad, one he shared with two other shadow presences. I heard that he had been selling opium. I had bumped into a school friend and drug buddy, Stu "Jimmy" Shand, walking down Morningside Road, stoned out of his mind. I hadn't ever tried opium. I wanted to.

After work I had taken a 16 bus all the way down to Elm Row at the top of Leith Walk. I had then called Ricey from a phone box. This is what you had to do. You dialed his number, let it ring three times, hung up, then called back and Ricey would answer. His paranoia was great: great enough to have cameras trained at his front doors round the clock, great enough to have most of Lothian and Borders Police ignoring every other crime just to listen in to Ricey's phone calls. His door would remain unanswered if you didn't call first, music was played at a very low volume, and his stash was secreted well, no one knew where.

As I was saying, soft yellow light and there were five of us, including me. The music played quietly on the turntable, "Another Green World" by Eno, with its serpentine slides and lazily challenged rhythms. I sat on the floor. Ricey sat on the sofa with an amazing-looking girl. She was so beautiful, half-hidden in the light, I kept staring at her. I think she had red hair, it was hard to tell, but it hung to her shoulders over a white t-shirt and denim jacket, a shiny black skirt, and black tights. I could not tell if she was Ricey's girlfriend or was with one of the other two who were here.

Monkey Wilson sat on the other side of the low coffee table from me with his grinning crony. I was scared of Monkey Wilson. He came from Oxgangs and Ali knew him, and had done, him and his crazy family, his entire life. "He's a fuckin' heedcase, man," Ali had warned me. "Just fuckin' snaps, same as a' the other Wilsons." His fights were legendary and his family was legendary: four brothers and a sister under one council roof with his parents. The entire family was a cottage industry of domestic break-ins, warehouse break-ins, auto theft, and anything else to supplement any number of social security fiddles they had going. Tonight he was mellow. Maybe he was with the girl. He was short, thick and ugly, a crop of tight brown curls on an oval face with no chin, a weak moustache, thick wet lips like two worms competing for his small round hole of a mouth. He had on shabby disco clothes, probably from somewhere like What Every Woman Wants on the Bridges, a schemey mecca of fire-hazard attire drawing its clientele from Craigmillar, Niddrie, Stenhouse and all the other little paradises dotted around Edinburgh's outskirts. His crony, all toothless idiotic grin and no words, sat leering at the girl, licking his lips every so often. I think I was high, I am sure everyone else was, I couldn't tell. I'd never tried opium. It was subtle. It sneaked through the back door into your mind. I had bought some from Ricey and immediately stoked a small pipe and passed it around.

Conversation was minimal but nothing was unusual; this was visiting your dealer, there was always a parade of disparate characters trickling in and out. Buy (after sitting and making empty pleasantries for a while, you couldn't just come out and say what you wanted), stay for a smoke, leave. It was busier at holidays and after droughts. I remember being at Colin's, sitting in his living room with twelve other people in a cloud of hash smoke.

"Did ye get that motorbike, Monkey?" Ricey asked, head tilted back slightly, half-shut eyes.

"Aye, but some cunt nicked it frae the front, outside ma hoose." Wet lips and a disgusted look.

"Probably selt it fur the parts, ye ken?" the crony piped up with a crude lisp.

"Aye, mebbe," Monkey said without patience indicating the crony with a sharp turn of the head.

A pause.

"Fuckin' out my heed, man," said Monkey.

"Aye, this is good stuff," said Ricey, turning to the girl. "You all right, Ailsa?"

"Yes, thanks," she whispered, silk brushing silk, a brilliant smile for a millisecond. I wanted her.

"Gonnae make us a cup ay tea, Ricey, aye?" Monkey's voice, a pigeon to her hummingbird.

Ricey exhaled, "Fuck's sake, all right," and he got up from the sofa to go into the kitchenette which adjoined the living room. Once the kitchen light was on, the room and its inhabitants became more apparent. The walls were bare except for a large, tattered poster advertising "Scary Monsters" by David Bowie. There was a tiny portable television, an electric heater sat awkwardly in the fireplace and a low, chipped coffee table which was the centrepiece.

The girl was a redhead and she was more beautiful in the light, what little there was. The others must have recognized her beauty because Monkey looked at her, lips in an "o" like a wet purple tire. "Like the smoke, hen, aye?" he asked, his words tumbling gracelessly from his mouth like dead fish from a bucket.

"Yeah, it's amazing." Her voice was sleek and hopelessly upper-class against the lower working-class growl of Monkey.

"So, where are ye frum?" he asked, his voice trying to sound cordial, but sounding wholly challenging.

"Um, I live near the West End." She was caught off-guard. I could see the warning lights going off in her head, frightened about betraying her class.

"Oh aye? Where?" Monkey was immediately interested.

"Just near Haymarket Station, you know?"

"Oh aye, right," Monkey paused. "So are ye gonnae invite us over fur our tea, aye?" He was jeering now. The crony offered up a raspy chuckle.

"Oh, I don't think you want my cooking!" she laughed nervously.

"Oh, she can't cook!" Monkey was speaking in a crude, mocking, upper-class accent. "Maybe we can get the maid to do it?"

There was a silence as the atmosphere of the room turned on its stomach. Ricey stopped what he was doing in the kitchen and looked into the living room. "Leave her alone, Monkey, aye?" he said, but the class division had been clearly made.

Monkey ignored him and looked at Ailsa, a disgusting grin on his wretched face. "Aye, mebbe we could dae somethin' else while we're waitin fur oor tea, what d'ye think, hen?" He raised his eyebrows from his piggy eyes, and thrust his right index finger back and forth through a loop made by his left hand thumb and index finger.

"Hey, leave her alone, let's just enjoy the smoke and talk about something else," I said.

"Shut up, you fuckin' poof!" he shouted at me, before I'd even finished the sentence. It was the same as a crack to the face.

"Monkey, fuck off and fuckin' stop shouting," Ricey spit through clenched teeth.

"Come on, sorry if I offended you, but can we not just be civil?" I said shakily.

Somehow I thought Monkey was getting up quickly to come over to me and shake my hand. Why did I think that? I then, in the next split, split second, thought he was simply leaving abruptly, but all of a sudden his knee was on my chest and he was pulling my hair, using it to strike the back of my skull on the floor. Ricey had pulled him off before I even had time to defend myself.

"Fuckin' see if the neighbours call the fuckin' polis? Eh? Fuckin' see if they call the polis 'cos you're acting like a STUPIT BASTARD, Monkey, we're a' goin' tae jail." Ricey pronounced "jail" like "jile." "D'ye ken that?" he hissed.

I stood up quickly. "Cheers Ricey," I said, "I'm away."

Ailsa rose as well. "Yes, me too." She looked at me. "I'll get you down the stairs."

The crony sat chuckling, thin, balding and toothless, his cruel eyes mocking. "Next time I see you, ya cunt," Monkey pointed at Ailsa, "You're FUCKED, fuckin' good and proper, fuckin' snobby dyke." He spat. "And you." He pointed at me. "Just fuckin' call an ambulance, ya wee fuckin' poof."

We walked hastily to the door and exited the flat, the sound of our shoes slap-slapping off the stairwell walls like some dwindling applause. We walked in silence down Montgomery Street to Elm Row. I was shaking and I was frightened that Monkey and his sidekick were following us. I realized that I'd forgotten the opium I'd bought from Ricey, it was sitting on the coffee table where I had left it, but I was certainly not about to go back for it. I looked to the side at Ailsa, all at once I saw her beauty and vulnerability and wanted to keep her safe. I took her hand, she squeezed mine, and right then, something changed. The fear was sluiced out of my system, the ugly loping terror chased out and replaced by warmth and sweetness.

Everything was going to be all right. We walked down Broughton Street, hand in hand, and took a left at the bottom, making our way into the New Town.

The night was warm and muggy, the sweetness of the well-kept New Town Gardens perfumed the air. Gliding: we were gliding along, the white streetlights, the opium, and the grey Georgian buildings made me feel like we were in a black-and-white film, a melodrama.

The kiss took place outside the Royal Circus, by the wrought-iron fence of a communal garden, a bush hanging over, under which we stood. We had stopped without saying a word, and looked at the Royal Circus bar. Perhaps she wanted to go in, perhaps I did, but all of a sudden my lips were on hers, and god, it was hungry, made so by the fright, by the fear, the wanting to pull beauty from behind the violent thing. I wanted to take her right there, my hand around her slim waist. She pushed my hand down gently, reading my thoughts and feeling me through my trousers.

"Let's just go for a drink, okay?" she indicated the bar with a slight gesture of her hand. "Do you like this dump?" she smiled.

"Yes, I like this dump." I said back, I actually liked it a lot more than I was going to let on, it was packed with the kind of upwardly mobile young things on whose coattails I was so happy to ride after leaving my supermarket every day.

We walked into the bar just as the first few droplets of rain were hitting the pavement and found two stools by the bar, even though it was quite busy. I was a soft ripple in a pool of clear water. The ugly, violent monster from Ricey's had been replaced with beauty.

"I left all that opium, but I'm not going back for it," I said as we sat down.

She pushed her hand through her vibrant hair and laughed. "Hadn't bought mine yet! Does that mean you're broke?"

"Well, yeah. I've got enough for a drink, I suppose."

"Let me get these. What d'you want?"

"Pernod and blackcurrant, please."

She raised her eyebrows at the same time she slipped a Du Maurier out of her cigarette packet and lit it with a black lighter. She exhaled smoke quickly and gracefully whilst addressing the girl behind the bar, "Pernod and blackcurrant, and I'll have a gin and tonic, please." She turned back to me. "Thanks for standing up for me. That bloke was frightening, really mental. Do you know him?"

"I've seen him around, here and there. He's from Oxgangs. I've got a friend from there who's known him his whole life, says he's a headcase, whole family's nuts. They're also thieves. I was worried you might give him your address."

"Oh, not likely," she said and touched my fingers lightly. "I might, might give it to you, though."

Our drinks were put down in front of us and Ailsa brought out a ten pound note from a small purse she had inside the green army bag she had been carrying.

"How do you know our friend, Ricey, then?" I asked.

She looked at me a little incredulously. "Same as you, I expect. Drugs, and that we rich kids from the private school sector need to stick together."

"Oh, I'm not rich," I said a little too quickly.

"You went to Heriot's, though, didn't you?"

I looked at her curiously. "How did you know that?"

She giggled. "I guessed. I'm right, aren't I?"

"Yes, you are." Were we that obvious? "I didn't pay fees, though. I had a scholarship."

I was half-lying, I had gone there as a fee payer until my dad had died, then there was no charge. Fatherless kids got to ride free of charge, something to do with the original intent and philosophy of the school.

She was wearing a subtle jasmine oil, probably bought from Cockburn Street Market. It was, along with her radiance, driving me to distraction. The kiss was barely enough, the red hair to just below her shoulders, her lips and intense eyes; maybe she saw the schoolboy lust in my eyes, because she pre-emptively redirected the conversation.

"Did he hurt you? That ape back at Ricey's?"

"No, it gave me a fright, that's all. Mental case."

"I was worried they'd follow us."

"Me too, but we're okay. I'm glad we're here, I feel kind of safe."

"Yeah, but it's the Circus. These kinds of places bore me to death, Adam. All these people here, they don't know what the fuck they want and they don't have to, really. They've got money and Daddy'll find them a good job working for his company. I'm looking for something amazing. I'm so bored I can barely move and this kind of place just irritates me."

I couldn't for the life of me remember my name being mentioned. I hadn't said it and I don't think Ricey had either, and Monkey and his crony didn't know it.

Maybe Ricey had said it during or just after the attack. Maybe he'd said, "All right, Adam, aye?" and maybe, right now, as I was drifting into love like a tiny boat on an enormous, calm sea. I didn't care.

"I'm dead serious, I'm so tired of banalities and niceties. I want my life to be amazing. I want miracles. And I am absolutely not going to have a boring life."

"All that stuff that happened at Ricey's wasn't exactly boring," I said.

"It was horrible, but you've got to admit, the adrenaline rush on top of the opium, fucking amazing!"

I shuddered, thinking of Monkey's prehistoric mouth, his meaty hands banging my head on the floor.

"I'm quite sure I'll be happy without seeing Monkey Wilson ever again," I laughed nervously.

"I'm sure," she said, taking my hand and casting her eyes down. "I just miss that feeling I had when I was six or seven, when I didn't know what was going to happen and these amazing miracles just seemed to happen. Then when I became a teenager, everything was just so, well, disappointing. I miss it so much."

"I can give you miracles, Ailsa, if that's what you would like. I'll give them to you every day." It came out of my mouth with no prior thought. It was lust and it was love. You could not—could not—look into that face without promising the world. You could absolutely not hold that hand or touch that skin without forgetting everything that had happened. Not possible. Her face betrayed little, but enough. I could see the surprise and the joy. I knew it, I had to have her.

"Well, hello Adam," she said. Leaning forward, she kissed me on the lips. "We are going to be very, very close, you and me." The effervescent warmth was like thousands of tiny hot bubbles making their way through my bloodstream, her face, again and again and again.

She took my hand in both of hers and rubbed the top. It tingled, like she was massaging an energy into me, her face calm.

"I'm not much of a joker," she said. "And if I have nothing to say, then I won't talk, and I never enter into anything lightly, Adam, ever."

I was unnerved, still recovering from the kiss, which was incredible, but I was stuck: was she winding me up, or had I opened a door that I perhaps should have waited to open?

What if she knew I worked in a supermarket? That I rang up old age pensioners who bickered with me about the price of tea every day? I suddenly burst out laughing; I laugh when nervous and I laugh at the gravest news.

"I'm sorry, I didn't mean to laugh. I mean, nothing's funny, I just…"

"It's okay, Adam. I like your laugh. I like it a lot." And I saw her smile again. It was the ocean parting to salute the sun. It was dawn at the roof of the world, the most radiant thing, I was suddenly completely humbled, and I was utterly in love.

"Do you care that I work in a supermarket? I ring up cross old ladies all day. It's horrible."

She said nothing, but pulled another cigarette out of her packet and lit it. "Why don't you meet me here tomorrow afternoon? About two, outside." She exhaled smoke and shook hair out of her eye.

I couldn't stop staring, and she didn't seem to notice. I was a bit disappointed. I wanted her to invite me to her flat. I didn't want to walk away from her. Maybe she would invite me. "I'm working until eight. I could meet you tomorrow night."

"Oh, call in, tell them your grandmother's dead or something."

"Okay, one dead grandmother coming up. Tomorrow at two."

We sat silently as she finished her cigarette. We then got up to leave together without exchanging words. We were completely synchronized with each other, both knowing there was nothing left to say. However, somewhere in the back of my mind it occurred to me to ask if I could just fast forward and go to her house now, but I restrained myself. Outside it was pouring down; we stood in the doorway and looked at it for a few minutes before I eventually lit a cigarette.

"You live near here, don't you—unless you were trying to throw Monkey way off?" I ventured.

"Yes, pretty near."

I was hoping that the torrential rain might steer her in the direction of inviting me to her place.

"I'm not going to invite you, not tonight, Adam."

"Which way are you walking? I could at least walk part of the way."

"Look, here." She pulled out a tiny notebook and a pencil from her bag, wrote her number on a page and tore it off, folding it, and giving it to me. "Now you," she said handing me the pencil. I tore off the bottom of the page she had handed me and wrote my phone number on it.

"Goodnight, Adam."

"Goodnight, Ailsa," I said and she took my chin in her hand and kissed me, then she walked down the stairs, waved without looking back and immediately hailed a passing cab. I said her name under my breath, thinking about the incredible island she was named after. I idly wondered why she had taken off like that. No romantic walk, not even the offer of a lift in the cab to the nearest bus stop. But none of this had been done with any selfishness I felt. She definitely had her reasons, and so be it.

Ailsa Craig, an awe inspiring rock that juts out of the Firth of Clyde about a thousand feet high. A mountain in the sea, made of granite and covered in gannets, gorgeous, and beautifully at odds with the dark, feline softness of Ailsa, my Ailsa.

I set off walking to the West End, glowing, and caring nothing about the heavy rain. I walked up Howe Street, high and electric in the rain. I kept thinking I saw her, and I kept thinking I saw Monkey and crony, hiding in doorways ready to mug me.

I ended up walking almost the whole way home. I just kept moving, Ailsa walking inside me. Ailsa Craig, rock in the sea, Ailsa Craig, rock in the sea, Ailsa Craig, rock in the sea. I played a game where I would try to stop thinking about her for as long as I could and then, when I couldn't stand it anymore, I would allow myself a look at her face or her hair or I would remember her smell or I would remember the way she said a certain word, a word like "Adam," the jagged ends of her hair brushing quickly across the top of her shoulders, her eyes dipping downwards.

I walked up the Mound and down George IV Bridge to the Meadows. There were a few bands of students out drinking, some backpackers looking lost and intrigued and wet. I left the path and walked over the muddy grass, eventually breaking into a run, running in the rain on the soft muddy ground took me away from the city and onto some giant and anonymous field outside of time. Running to Ailsa.

I reached Morningside and my street quickly, it seemed. The whole journey taken up with Ailsa's beauty, nothing left to think about.

I was tired and jittery. My street was deathly quiet, it usually was; a small cul-de-sac where I had lived with my mother for a couple of years. It was not the house I grew up in; that had been larger, but we had stayed there long after my father had left, enduring a year-round freezing darkness and suffocating silence where I learned to make myself scarce.

Moving into a smaller flat had done very little to dissipate the freezing darkness and silences I lived in. But I had bought, with my own money, a decent record player and used it to drown out the silence with Echo and the Bunnymen, Josef K, and Simple Minds, amongst other things. My mother worked part-time in the admissions office of the Princess Margaret Rose Hospital, which was not far away. It meant she was home much too often for my liking.

I opened the front door to the muffled sounds of late-night television coming from the living room.

"One of your friends phoned you. Bloody nerve calling at this hour." She made no attempt to hide her disdain. "Probably that stupid girl you used to see."

"What did she say, Mum?"

"I don't know, I didn't answer it."

"How did you know it was for me?"

"Well it wasn't for me, was it? And it wasn't for your bloody father," she said as if it was that obvious and I was that stupid.

"I'm going to my room," I said flatly.

In my room I turned on the bedside lamp and started to peel off my sodden clothes when the phone started to ring. I jumped into the hall without my shirt.

"I'll get it, Mum, it's probably that stupid girl I used to see," I said blithely and picked up the phone.

"Hello?"

"Hello, Adam, it's Ailsa."

"Ailsa," I said, because saying it was like unwrapping a gift over and over again.

"Listen, why don't you just come to my house tomorrow, that's where I was going to take you anyway. Come at two and I'll make you lunch. Palmerston Place, 21, do you know how to find it?"

"Oh yes, no problem."

"Two it is."

"Can't wait."

"Neither can I. Good night, angel," and she hung up.

Good night, angel. The words slammed into me like an express train made of rose petals. I was dizzy and quickly went to my room to sit down.

I took off my wet trousers and slipped into a pair of gym shorts I took from a drawer, lighting a cigarette. I thought about her address, Palmerston Place, just west of the West End. The houses around there were spectacular, and its proximity to the City Centre had to mean that she probably still lived with her probably wealthy parents.

Ailsa. Ailsa Craig, the awe inspiring rock sticking out like a god in the Firth of Clyde.

Ailsa and Adam, Celtic, biblical. I played back her beauty in my head and invented her mystery. I put on a classical piano record and continued to smoke and build my Ailsa with the fortification of my incredible imagination. I didn't usually listen to classical, but it draped the room in wonder and tranquillity at the same time. It was perfect, weaving its mysteries and questions around me. I realized I was very nervous about the following day. Two in the afternoon was an insurmountable climb. I had to call work and lie before I did anything. Then what? Wait? Hide? I lived so near the supermarket that any declarations of illness would have to be backed with physical evidence as I invariably bumped into someone I worked with if I set foot outside the flat.

I got up from my bed and picked up a pad of A4 paper and a pen from on top of my chest of drawers. I sat down cross-legged on my bed with the pad on my knees and began to write:

My dearest Adam,

I do hope you don't mind my writing to you so quickly after first meeting you, but I think we met in such an unusual way, I feel like you are so close to me right now, tonight, but so far away! I just can't wait until I see you tomorrow, I can't wait to sit down and talk to you and find out who you are, this magical man who came to my rescue and kissed me underneath the dangling bush outside the Royal Circus!

I can't wait to show you what I can give and do for you, my sweetness, of how complete I can make you feel, how high I can make you fly, and how completely scandalous it's all going to be!! And maybe how one day we can both run away together to Amsterdam or Cyprus? Or just Glasgow, who cares! All that matters is that now I've found you, I'm never going to let you go, my Adam. Never.

I am kissing this paper all over for you in the hope that you will dream of nothing but me tonight and all nights.

Goodnight, my love.
Your sweet angel,
Ailsa

I looked at it briefly and then ripped the page from the pad and started again.

My Adam,

I'm angry at you! Yes, angry at you for not making me take you home to mine tonight. For not making me show you how good I feel in all the right places, for not making me strip in front of you, for not making me lower myself onto your hard prick, letting my red hair tickle your neck as I bounce up and down on top of you. Just you wait, you are not going to believe what I am capable of, Adam, but you're going to have to wait until tomorrow!!

Think about me tonight, but don't dare touch yourself, I'll know!
Your new toy,
Ailsa

I read over my letter to me from her, feeling myself grow, I started to kiss the paper the way she would kiss the paper, strong and soft, strong and soft. I came, barely touching myself, and then quickly fell into a deep sleep.

The next morning I was woken, wrenched out of a deep sleep, by the radio in the kitchen blaring Radio One to the point of distortion. I was on top of the bed, the pad of paper and the letters beside me. I exclaimed slightly, looking at the letters and then tearing them up quickly. The radio at deafening volume was a favoured tactic of my mother's to either get me up, or, more commonly as a weapon in the ongoing war she was waging against the upstairs neighbours, a frequently revolving collective of Napier College students who had all incurred the wrath of Margret Kelvin within a week of moving in. This had all started when one of their number, who had moved out a long while back, had come home drunk and loud from the pub one night, waking my mother and beginning her very one-sided campaign of perpetual penalization.

I would see them occasionally outside the flat, or more frequently at work where they would come through my checkout to purchase their staples of wine and biscuits. At one time, there was a particularly beautiful female living up there. I had an intense crush on her and one late afternoon as she was walking past my checkout, I called her over. I introduced myself and apologized for my mother's unreasonable behaviour. "She's mental, and I'm really embarrassed about her," I said, looking into her silky feline eyes. She broke into a smile, "Don't worry, Adam. I know she's got it in for us all, but she is your mum, isn't she? I'm off to grab a bottle of wine!" adding, "Oh, I'm Jenny!" and spinning off to the wines and spirits department.

In the kitchen, it was a familiar scene when I got up. My mother, her back to me, was pouring boiling water into a cup, seemingly oblivious to the distorted music haemorrhaging from the ancient radio on the countertop. "They kept me up all bloody night again, playing records and television until all hours." There was a familiar bitter edge to her enraged voice. It frightened me. I had known it my whole life. It meant that with very little provocation, she would explode into a dreadful rage. Sometimes I would steal quietly away and sometimes, I would push it, making it burst so that it would be over with. Then I would steal away.

"Mum, I live here too. I didn't make any noise, but you woke me up." It was futile to tell her that the upstairs neighbours had, in fact, made none or little noise at all. "Could you not turn it down now? You've made your point."

"You don't have a say in this house until you chip in for your keep."

I felt an anger rise in me, my teeth clenched, and my lips tightened.

"I'm saving up so I can get the fuck out of your little concentration camp, don't worry."

"Don't you dare speak to me like that, wasting your life going out every night. How much have you saved?"

Her temper was lost, face mottled and red. Mine too, was lost. I had not saved a penny, of course, and I walked slowly, shaking, towards the radio, picked it up and slammed it hard down on the counter. There was immediate silence

"You're fucking insane," I said quietly.

"I am not insane!" she screamed, like an animal. I looked at her gaping mouth and wide eyes and was repulsed. The words had come out of my mouth without my being aware. All I could feel were my fingernails digging harshly and deeply into my palms.

"I am not insane, I am not insane, I am not insane, I am not insane," I said, mocking her, over and over, quietly and between gritted teeth to myself as my blood pressure rose and I felt myself perspire and go deep red. She stood looking at me with the same open mouth, horror, anger and possibly fear making up her hideous mask. I stopped. I had things to do, I did not want this ugly, hot, red event on me anywhere when I went to see Ailsa. What did I have to do before I saw my love again?

I had to call work. I had to call in ill. I walked out of the kitchen closing the door, and picked up the phone, which was on a wire just long enough that you could take it into the cupboard in the hall for a little privacy. I had to speak to the staff supervisor, a humourless old woman by the name of Jess, whose poker face never cracked. Calling up to miss a shift was never easy; she punctuated the calls with enough silences to make you very uncomfortable. As I dialled the number, I realized that I didn't have a good story. What would I tell her that didn't sound like a dreadful lie? The only thing I had in my favour was that she did have a soft spot for me—at least, as close to a soft spot as she could have, granting me lenience on several occasions before.

"Yes, Adam?" she demanded coldly as I told her who was calling. I had an idea.

"Jess, I had a wee accident. I fell off a ladder at home and I've sprained my wrist. I had to go to casualty last night and I'm not to move my fingers for a few days. I've got it in a splint. "

There was a long pause, a cool rushing of dead air on the line punctuated by crackles, and the distant sounds of the supermarket at work. Eventually, a sigh.

"If it's no any better by Monday, ye'll need tae get a line from your doctor," she stated stonily. I could see her face in my mind: beady, black eyes in an angry, round, white, pudding face under a black and grey permed mess.

"I've got an appointment to see him first thing on Monday morning. My shift doesn't start until the afternoon. I should be fine."

Another pause, another sigh.

"Right you are, then, son."

"I'll see you on Monday, Jess. Thanks, and I'm sorry for the inconvenience."

I put the receiver down and opened the cupboard door. My mother was standing there, staring wide-eyed with a look of horror on her red face.

"You have no trouble lying through your teeth, do you?"

"It's none of your business. I need the day off." Then, another flash of inspiration. "I have a job interview. It's at the Caledonian Hotel, full-time job. I couldn't very well call up and ask for the day off to look for a better job, could I?"

She turned and walked back into the kitchen, pausing in the doorway to turn and deliver her parting line. "I think it is very sad what has happened to us. I think it is very sad the way you lie." This was spoken in her defeated martyr voice, a quiet sing-song voice reserved for speaking about the injustices inflicted upon her.

"Right, Mum," I said and went into the bathroom to find the necessary things I would need with which to make a splint for my "injured" wrist. I found a bandage, some safety pins, and then in the kitchen I found a small white plastic spatula.

I had lied my whole life, to her anyway, and had found it by far the best way to navigate through my time with her, her obsessive and relentless spying, complaining and nagging.

6 · Q QUARTERS

It was 8:30 in the morning. I had until 2 pm and lived far too near work to be able to roam the streets of Morningside without being spotted by a co-worker. Of course, having a bandaged arm granted me a certain clemency, but I certainly didn't feel like explaining myself or having some eagle-eyed busybody spotting that the nurse in the casualty had resorted to a plastic spatula to straighten and immobilize my wrist. I certainly couldn't stay at home, so I picked out the nicest clothes I had: a slightly ill-fitting, two-piece suit I had bought at a vintage shop in the Grassmarket and a green cotton shirt from the same place. It was the best I could do, the question of 'what would Ailsa like?' hanging over me, intimidating and thrilling at the same time. I dressed and put the splint on in my room. It was not easy. I had to wrap the bandage around my wrist keeping the spatula in place with two fingers of the same hand. It got easier with the more bandage I rolled until eventually I could pull it tightly into place and secure it with safety pins.

Finally, I was ready to leave and sat on my bed straining to hear exactly where my mother was in the house, not wishing to encounter her on my way out. Utter silence. She may have been lying down. My whole childhood was sprinkled with memories of her lying down in her darkened room and demanding silence. I opened my door and quickly walked to the front door, exiting quietly.

I took a left at the end of my street. This meant I was heading away from the town centre where I eventually wished to be but, as I had hours to kill, I didn't mind going miles out of my way to guarantee my not running into anyone I knew, even though I had a rock solid excuse. It felt so stupid wearing a plastic spatula under a bandage. What if it slipped out? I didn't feel particularly inconspicuous.

I decided to head over to Craiglockhart, a quiet area next to Morningside, and make my way downtown from there. I took a right down Balcarres Street, the silence of Morningside stifling me. No traffic, just the menacing presence of electrical hum. I reached the number 23 bus terminus, pausing to look at the lamppost graveyard: a workyard packed with retired city streetlights, both ornate and plain, awaiting refurbishment or different fates, huge lampheads strewn around the tarmac. I had never seen anyone working or moving inside.

"Adam!" The sound hung in the air like a sculpture in the bright morning air, complicated, curved clear glass, the crystalline voice of Jackie. "What have you done to your hand?" she asked, concern in her voice as she crossed the street.

She was wearing shorts and a white t-shirt. I forgot that she ran here every morning. You really can't walk anywhere in Morningside, or Edinburgh for that matter, without bumping into someone you know. I was panicked; I didn't want Jackie to know what I was doing. I didn't want anyone to know what I was doing. Ailsa was my hidden jewel in a box.

"It's nothing, really. I had to get out of work today, I wanted to go fishing with Moggy and DeMarco so I called in and said I'd sprained my wrist. Had to make it look real!"

"Where's your rod, then?" she asked.

"I thought you knew, Jackie!"

We both laughed at the innuendo.

"I'm borrowing one. I don't actually own a fishing rod." I didn't really need to lie to her. Was it because she looked like she'd be hurt? Because I couldn't help it?

"I'm a little bit late actually, Jackie."

She cocked her head very slightly to the side, giving me an almost imperceptible look that could have equally been sizing up my looks or my honesty. She took a step towards me and cupped the side of my face with her right hand, putting her lips softly on mine. Her kiss was full but spectral, a sexual ghost moving through me sending currents of energy spreading through my limbs. She softly pulled away.

"Have a good day with the boys," she said, a very slight irony inflecting the word "boys."

"If you don't catch anything, I'll be home all day." At this, she turned on her heel and started jogging again, turning around to grin and wink as I stood there watching her.

I was unsettled by the incident. It was hot and I continued walking, my mind on Ailsa but with the sweet ghost of me and Jackie drifting through my thoughts. The kiss worried me. My lips throbbed where it had been, as if they had grown redder and plumper and anyone who saw me, especially Ailsa, would know that I had been kissed, my lips glowing as red as a warning sign.

I wound through the small, curling streets that moved between George Watson School's playing fields and the grounds of the Royal Edinburgh Hospital—the Royal Ed, as it was called—a psychiatric hospital, or looney bin, as it was commonly known. I had known a few of my peers to end up there, mostly from school or from similar, fee-paying rich backgrounds that my friends and I had associated with. I naturally had drifted towards a small subculture of drug users, hash and acid mainly, and a couple of poor souls had ended up "acid casualties" and been admitted to the Royal Ed. This served as a cautionary tale to all: if we weren't careful we'd end up in the Royal Ed.

Along the way, there were a few people out tending small but dense gardens. The air was thick with the lazy hysteria of stimulated bees flitting from flower to flower, their buzzing, zigzagged across the morning air. There were distant sounds of lawnmower engines being started and their low drones were loping giants compared to the sharp focus of the sound of the bees' wings.

Jackie had seemed vulnerable and I now felt badly. But she was fine, she was always fine, a little highly strung at times, but nowhere near as highly strung as I was. She could be, as my lips were now testament to, wonderfully unpredictable though.

I walked down a steep street and realized how far she ran every morning, from her house on Newbattle Terrace, around the north end of Watson's, down Colinton Road and then across a little, so that she got a stretch of the Union Canal running south. Then crossing back over Colinton Road at Meggetland (the sports grounds belonging to Boroughmuir School) to run up the steep hill that I was now walking slowly down.

I decided to walk alongside the canal for a stretch. I used to spend a lot of my time walking or cycling down the canal, usually with Moggy. It went from scenic to claustrophobic and industrial very quickly and then back again. At Meggetland, going north, there were the playing fields then the pleasant wooded greenery of Harrison Park which quickly turned into the narrow dark corridor where you were dwarfed by the black backs of tenements leading up to the colossus of the Scottish & Newcastle Brewery.

We used to set off homemade explosives around there, Moggy and I. The loud cracks would ricochet off the flat tenement backs, bringing startled faces to kitchen windows.

One bored Saturday morning, we shocked ourselves. We had made a small explosive out of a pressurized container of gas for a camping stove smothered in some kind of flammable glue for an accelerant. We were just a little south of Meggetland, and the explosion was a lot louder and more spectacular than we had expected, creating a quick black and orange mushroom cloud that dissipated into black smoke that hung stunned in the air like some giant insect, frozen. Moggy and I had sat in astonished, unmoving silence, hidden in the bushes as all around us thousands of birds screamed their fear. As the bird sound began to dissipate, it was overtaken by a low rumble, getting quickly louder as we were narrowly missed by a terrified, wild-eyed horse galloping past us at unimaginable speed.

Very shaken, we walked slowly north on the towpath and about a half-mile or so later, we saw a small cluster of people. As we approached, we saw that they were gathered around a girl of about thirteen or fourteen, a black velvet riding helmet on her head, her riding clothes muddied. She was chalk white and looked very shocked, her breathing short and fast. She kept asking about the horse.

"Try no tae move, hen, there's an ambulance coming," a young woman said in a soothing tone, bent down beside the girl.

"We heard a gun or something," I said, not believing my morbid nerve.

"I don't know son, but ye'd better move along, there's not that much room on the path for the ambulance crew," said an older man in his mid-forties with a newspaper under his arm.

We walked on in silence for a while until Moggy started giggling and singing "Crazy horses, waaa, waaa!"

"Fuckin' hell, Moggy, that's no funny!"

"Och, she'll be all right and they'll find the stupid horse."

"She could have fallen in the canal and drowned. What if she'd died?"

"Aye well, she didnae, did she?"

"I suppose so."

We walked on for a minute or so before we both started singing "Crazy horses, waaa, waaa!"

That must have been about four or five years ago now. There had been no repercussions from our behaviour. We had walked away from it free. I don't know whatever happened to the horse or the girl, I never read the local papers.

I walked past the top edge of Craiglockhart Pond, the wooded hill that served as the grounds for the Royal Ed, looming over, dense and steep. I walked up Colinton Road to the Meggetland Bridge that crossed the canal and I continued north on the towpath. Scattered dog walkers and joggers enjoyed the summer morning. I was kicking myself for wearing the clothes I had chosen. I had taken the jacket off but the trousers felt heavy and woollen. My legs were sweating and very uncomfortable and it would be hours before I could conceivably remove them, assuming that Ailsa would let me remove them. I decided to just make my way to her area now and stay there. I wanted to walk where she walked, I had to look. Then I would while away the rest of my time in the botanical gardens.

I walked quickly through the West End, through Stockbridge to the botanical gardens, quite a walk, really. When I got there, I went straight to the Henry Moore. "Reclining Figure" had obsessed me since I was a baby. I was transfixed by its casual violence, the sleek, black horror, the unassuming disfigurement.

It was easy to spend hours in the botanics. Steep paths, shrouded in intimate foliage leading to secret green corners. Gigantic, antiquated wrought-iron terrariums housing outlandish and regal trees, dry, humid, dry. When I was very young, I used to run ahead of my mother and father to hide under a favourite weeping willow by a pond. Its long, graceful tendrils hung so low as to create a living green curtain that met the short, well-kept grassy floor.

This was purgatory and paradise. I walked the paths. Occasional walkers and a band of children were all I encountered. I kept superimposing my image of Ailsa in these gardens. I closed my eyes and inhaled the syrupy complex perfumes.

Ailsa and I walking here in the mornings.

Ailsa and I watching a swan tend to its cygnets.

Ailsa and I walking in the post-coital dusk, covertly, informed only by our own world, heady wine making us clumsy in our search for a place to make love in the grassy labyrinth, languidly and sweetly in the dusky ghosts of perfume.

Eventually, time passed. The one o'clock gun sounded and cut the day in two, for me, separating the stresses of the morning with the promise of the afternoon and evening. The one o'clock gun was a small cannon fired from Edinburgh Castle every day, used as a means to give the ships in Leith Harbour an accurate time check.

The sky was being covered by early afternoon cloud, piece by piece as the sun was slowly obscured, bringing the temperature down and giving me some comfort and relief and making my walk more pleasant. At one point, I took off my shoes and let my feet dangle in the cool water of a pond. It was then I realized that it was probably all right to take off my bandage. I removed it and rolled it up in my jacket pocket.

I walked slowly to the address she had given me. It was torture, but I managed somehow to show up at her house at five to two, and not twenty past one. She was standing at the gate, her big, intelligent eyes smiling at me, her red hair in a ponytail revealing her chalk-white neck plunging into a t-shirt and jeans.

"Hello, Adam. You found me, yeah?"

"Oh, yes, no problem."

"Come here, then."

She held out her hand and I took it. She led me down the path by the side of the house which took you to the back garden. The house was enormous looking and I couldn't tell if it was divided into flats, or if she still lived with her parents. The path turned into a short flight of five steps which took you to a red door, a basement door which faced onto the garden. The garden was long, the far wall facing the building was a well-kept tangle of bushes and flowers.

"This is where I live," she said as she opened the basement door. "Mum and my stepdad live upstairs. Come in."

The door opened into a spacious living room. I noticed a vivid-blue painted bathroom on my right, and, facing me at the other end of the living room on the right, a spiral staircase.

"The stairs go up to their kitchen. Well, actually, it's my kitchen too, I don't have one down here, but they never come down and I can just go up there and help myself to whatever I need. There's a door at the top, they can't hear me."

This was all volunteered by way of an explanation that I did not ask for or need, but I smiled and squeezed her hand.

"I was waiting for you outside so you didn't have to go upstairs and ring the front door bell. You don't want to have to meet my mum, I mean, she's fine, but, you know, well, I just wanted to grab you first," she smiled.

Orange and blue walls and Habitat furniture exuded a post-1970s Bohemian affluence. There were a few scattered cushions on the floor, and on one wall, a long low table boasting an incredible turntable and speakers. Opposite the stereo was a large double futon bed covered in a multicoloured bedspread.

The centrepiece of the living room was a huge framed reproduction of Matisse's "The Red Studio" which glared out from above a long sofa, draped in a yellow and gold tapestry. There were a couple of lamps, as well as a few candles stuck in wine bottles on the shiny light hardwood floor—bare, save for a patterned dark red rug.

The opposite end of the basement flat boasted three huge windows in a wide alcove that faced onto the wall of the space that separated the building from the street and pavement. In the alcove was a wooden chair and a small desk. On the desk were several sticks of charcoal and a half-finished drawing on paper of an old man's face.

"Not much of a view out there I'm afraid," she said quietly, "You see a lot of ankles and knees. Oh, take off your shoes, relax. Do you want to take a shower? You can if you want."

"Actually, yes, that would be great. Are you sure your mum won't come down?"

"Oh, god no! She knows better. Hang on a sec." She climbed the spiral staircase and disappeared. I wondered if I should have declined the offer of a shower? It didn't seem to faze her. Perhaps it was obvious that I had been walking around in the sun all morning, perspiring through heat and nerves.

She came downstairs with a huge towelling robe over her arm. "One of my stepdad's old dressing gowns," she said giving it to me. I noticed the breast pocket had the insignia of an expensive hotel.

"Have a shower. I'll make some lunch for us—I did invite you for lunch, didn't I?" she smiled slyly.

"I... don't remember. All I remember is your address," I smiled.

The cool blue of the bathroom was peaceful. I heard some music starting as I stripped, the massaging surrealism of Debussy, piano dappling through the rooms at low volume. The bathroom was longer than it was wide, a narrow table against the wall with a vase of fuchsias and a small brass Buddha on it, a small wooden chair tucked under. There was a Picasso poster on the wall, curled with steam. I turned on the shower and stripped. The shower was powerful, not at all what I was used to, the impotent hand-held hose at my mother's.

I lifted my face and let the spray cascade over my skin. The soap was luxurious and smelled of summer. The Debussy music was playful in the distance.

When I eventually pulled the shower curtain back, I was startled to see Ailsa sitting at the chair. Anything strange about this silent action was offset by her beauty. She handed me a huge towel. "I wanted to be here while you showered. I hope you don't mind," she said solemnly.

"No, of course not, not at all," I said, although I was at once flustered, awestruck, and somewhat flattered. I vigorously dried and put the robe on.

"So, have you been out all morning?" she asked.

"Yeah, I lied to work and I left the house early. My mother was driving me mad."

"Did you tell work you'd broken your wrist or arm or something?"

"I said I'd sprained my wrist. How do you know?"

"There's a bandage and a plastic spatula sticking out of your jacket pocket." She started laughing and put her arms gently round my neck and began kissing me. I felt my body respond and she led me out of the bathroom and onto her bed.

She pulled off the crocheted bedspread and carelessly threw it on the floor without taking her eyes or mouth off me. She then pulled off the robe I was wearing, and took her own clothes off.

My hands took over, and her face became pure empathy as I pushed her red hair out of the way, my fingers lightly touching and caressing her bone structure underneath the skin, as soft as the spectre of petals. The skin on my hands tingled with a joyous electricity, closed eyes and liquid lips. My hand moved down her side to her waist and we lay down.

Her scent was subtle and enigmatic, ingeniously complex, a soft passage of sun and earth leading to the slightest sweetness. As I inhaled it from her neck, her skin was hot and cool at the same time and her fingers tenderly pushed and pulled at my spine and shoulders, solid and liquid endlessness, diving, entering. She whispered shapes of words, warm air in my mouth, the tongue like tide, walking through waves as every window in the world opens and shouts, the panorama of sweet suddenness and sadness, the melancholy of unanswered worship, the unattainable. I thrust deep as I heard her golden sighs. Then it is done, absolute drama and resolve.

When I woke, her head was on my chest and she woke up too. I saw her tangled hair and one open eye smiling at me, her thigh across my groin, pressing my spent cock into my lower stomach, her arm around my shoulder. She squeezed me. There was a sound on the pavement outside of kids running and shouting. I could not stop looking at her face, partially obscured by hair, her beauty as complex as her scent. I couldn't take it in at once and accept it, I had to look at parts of her and try and compile it and process it in my mind.

"I'm on the pill," she said and prised herself off me slowly, picking up a thin robe from the ground beside the bed and putting it on. "Come here," she said, cocking her head in the direction of the other end of the large room. I got up and stretched, picking up the robe she had given me.

"I'll be back in two shakes," she said and walked quickly up the spiral staircase.

I stood, dizzy and in a kind of sugary shock until she came back down the stairs with a baguette under one arm, a small container of Boursin, and a bottle of white wine. She set these things down on the rug on the floor and took a butter knife out of her pocket.

"Picnic," she said and disappeared up the stairs again, reappearing seconds later with two glasses.

I could not really speak. I couldn't quantify or qualify anything really, the superlatives I had were meagre to what her worth was. Surely she had heard the same from other lovers before me? I could not see why I had been chosen.

She walked over to the record player and put on something else. Edith Piaf. It blended into the afternoon beautifully. I uncorked the wine and poured it and we ripped off chunks of baguette and spread them with Boursin, the polite sweetness of the wine coupling perfectly with the sharp lemony boisterousness of the soft cheese.

"My mum paints, my stepdad's a lawyer," she said, answering the inevitable question I had not asked. "They gave me this flat for my fifteenth birthday. I knew they were converting it into something, workmen back and forth all day, but, my god, when they took me down here on my birthday at breakfast, I couldn't believe it."

"It's amazing," I said. "I live in a wee flat with my mum."

"You can stay here any time you like, Adam."

"Thanks, my work's up near where I stay."

"Do you like your work?" she asked.

"I fuckin' hate it."

"So, give it up."

"I need the money. I need to do something."

"What if I look after you? You won't need money, the fridge upstairs is always full."

"It's an okay job for just now, I suppose."

"I don't think you should go back."

Silence.

"I don't think I should go back, either."

The next twenty-four hours passed in what felt like an hour. We made love hungrily, then lazily. We grew sore but it was not enough to stop us. The ache turned into a sting and then turned into a white hot yearning as I would plunge into her. We came quickly and then slept for a few minutes or, occasionally, we'd smoke and pass a bottle of wine between us before doing it again. We had been listening to Schubert's piano sonatas at a low volume on the stereo; the music hung languidly like a gossamer tapestry over everything in the room.

Ailsa rose reluctantly and went upstairs, retrieving some grapes and mangoes. It must have been two in the morning. We sat in the bed making a mess with the mango pulp and passing the wine bottle back and forth. Dozing off again, we woke up possibly at six. There was a thin seam of light around the blackout blinds. Ailsa got up and drew a bath.

"Come on," she said, poking her tousled head out of the bathroom. As I walked over to the bathroom, she was in the steaming water. "I sting," she said "God, I sting! So worth it," she said and I lowered myself in.

"Ouch! You weren't kidding, were you?" I laughed as the hot water reached my genitals. I felt a very acute stinging as well. "Hope it goes away so we can do it again soon," I muttered.

"Oh, it will, angel, don't worry. If not, I'll just very carefully suck you off," she laughed.

I looked into her dark eyes; her smile was loving compassion. Every time I saw her face I would break down inside, so lovely it was.

"Adam, stay here with me and there will be no time, I don't even think I own a clock or a watch. We can be *enfants terrible*."

"What about..." I motioned upstairs with an upwards nod of my head.

"They don't care," she said shaking her head slightly. "Wait there." And she got out of the bath, springing naked and soapy into the living room. She came back with a joint and a cigarette lighter. She got back into the water, muttering a quiet "ouch" as she did so.

She lit the joint and inhaled deeply. "Nepalese, it's brilliant." She exhaled the pungent smoke into my face, breaking into a grin. "It's really lovely out. Let's smoke this and go for an adventure or something."

She passed the joint to me and I inhaled, relishing the dark, earthy taste in my mouth. "All right, that'd be great, an adventure—we could build a treehouse or a gang hut!"

She flicked water on me with her fingers lightly and giggled. We sat for a while in the bath, my legs encircling hers under the water. Occasionally my feet would massage her buttocks in the warm silence. Sometimes she felt there and not there, such was her softness in the warmth of the water. She reciprocated by using her toes to gently massage my genitals in the water, playfully, arousing me and reminding me of the glorious ache I felt.

I was coming in and out of consciousness: the joint and the warm water allowing me to drift into watery, sunshine-inflected dreams; the gentle massaging of my groin bringing me back again.

"Come on, sleepy, let's go for a walk. It'll do you good," she said and got out of the bath in one quick movement, like she'd been bracing herself for it. I followed her lead and jumped out. I was far more stoned than I thought I was and the room reeled before my eyes. I steadied myself against the wall and laughed.

"Are you okay?" she said, grabbing my arm.

"That was really strong hash," I exhaled.

"Plenty more where that came from. I've got a quarter."

I took a towel and dried myself, the power of the joint eventually settling into the beauty of everything around me and invigorating the euphoria I had been feeling for hours. The back and forward motion of the towel felt good and I threw on yesterday's clothes.

She stood in the middle of the living room. She had on tight blue jeans and was putting on a well-cut white chemise, leaving the top buttons open. She had pinned her hair up. She looked beautiful and I wanted her again. I stopped myself and she saw it in my eyes.

"Walk first, yeah?" she said quietly, smiling.

She had two pears, a ready rolled joint, a bottle of wine, and something else wrapped in newspaper which she put into a leather school satchel.

"*Allons-y!*" she said cocking her head in the direction of the door, and we left her flat. It was an incredible morning, bright, warm and still; an earthy, floral scent hung almost imperceptibly in the air, just there for us two. It was a quick walk and we were very soon sat down by the water of Leith at the Dean Village.

The bright sun played vivaciously off the moving water, sending arcs and flashes of light as if someone had made a film of everything in the world that was bright, flicking and sending to me messages of hope and happiness.

Ailsa reached into the satchel and pulled out the newspaper parcel. Opening it, I saw that it was a hollow turquoise glass phrenology head. She held it up to the sun. "Doesn't it look amazing? Isn't it so beautiful?" she turned it slowly, holding it against the sun and then the light from the river. "I just brought it to look at, but I bet if you asked it a question, it'd answer!" she giggled.

And why should I go back to work? Was this not complete tranquillity? Under a tree, twigs and branches netting the sky pell-mell from where we lay on the ground looking up, passing the glass head to one another to look through, the occasional crow caw-cawing, ricocheting against Edinburgh's urban beauty.

The river's mad but subtle conversation with itself was light and warmly reproachful and forgiving, reminding me of the Schubert that had so recently permeated our night and our lovemaking.

The day lazily embraced us. We heard some kids and a dog. We ate our pears noisily, slugged back some wine, then we smoked another joint.

"Mum and my stepdad will probably go away for the weekend. They've got a cottage near Galashiels so we can go upstairs if we want. Actually, we can do anything we fucking like, really—we can fuck our brains out in their bed, or on the dining room table, what d'you think?" She took my hand and stood up, and, rewrapping the glass head, she put it in the satchel and we made our way back home.

On the way back, our tranquillity was interrupted by a loud and vicious argument, between a man and a woman, standing on the pavement on Chester Street, their raw voices echoing and fraught, so aggravated that it was impossible to discern their words to tell what they were arguing about, save for a peppering of expletives. Every few seconds there seemed to be a menacing pause, pregnant with malice as each waited for the other's next move, waited for the answer to an accusation, for a justification, a gathering of enormous energies, ready for the next volley.

"I don't want to walk past it," said Ailsa, forcefully, and frightened, her voice taking on the slightest shade of a child's.

"Okay, let's just cross the road," I said.

"No, no, let's turn back and go down to West Maitland Street and around," she said, again, forcefully, like she was giving an order. Now the slightest shade of hysteria, she squeezed my hand tightly and I knew to just follow the direction.

The couple were a good enough distance away that it was hard to see what they were like except for being male and female. This was made easy by the harsh contrast in their voices: the man, a barking, spitting punch of a voice; the woman, a screaming, unstable saw. They were paused as if in mid-walk to face each other, as if what they had been arguing about whilst walking had suddenly grown by such incredible proportions as to make any more forward motion impossible and ludicrous save for the strange dance of sudden movements as they fought. There was no one else on the street, which made the whole thing in this glorious morning light akin to a showdown in a western movie.

Ailsa and I walked back to the house at a wordless, fast-paced clip. I could tell that the incident had upset her greatly and I wondered of the depth of someone's empathy, her empathy; it almost crushed me to see her this thrown, this wild-eyed and scared. I remembered that we had smoked a lot of strong hash and we had spent the night fucking so much that we had not slept, but witnessing the fight threw our timeless and heavenly sojourn into a buried corner, replacing it with a vivid and ugly human reality, making the sweetness of the memory of our lovemaking seem like a made-up tale.

We got into the flat and she immediately shuttered the windows, huge folding wooden shutters that were far more effective than curtains. She turned on her bedside lamp. "Let's just lie down and sleep for a while, okay?"

When I awoke, it was from a deep sleep, a thick black pause in the day, so thick that I had no concept of time. The room was pitch black, and there was no clock, so I lay there.

I could feel Ailsa beside me, and she surprised me by speaking. "It's nice to not know the time," she said quietly.

"Are you all right?" I asked. There was a long pause, followed by a sigh in the darkness.

"Those two fighting," she said, "That was Mum and my stepdad."

"Oh, fuck, oh, Ailsa, fuck—is it a regular occurrence?" I felt immediately stupid about the pointlessness of this question. What did it matter? It had happened, it had happened today, and it had devastated her.

"Well, put it this way: it wasn't an altogether altruistic move that they built me my own little lair down here away from them. They feel badly about fighting, and the ironic thing is that I can still hear them, loud and clear, even if they are all the way upstairs. Out of sight, out of mind, I suppose. I mean, what's good for them is that they don't know really if I'm in or out, less guilt to feel, and I just shut up about it. It's nice having all this for nothing; it's been this way since I moved down here two years ago."

"Why do they fight?" Again, another pointless question.

"I don't know, they just... goad each other. Why does anyone fight? They don't agree? I don't know, I wish you hadn't seen it, I wish you hadn't fucking heard it, it shakes me so."

I pulled her close.

"I think they're gone now, they have a cottage in the middle of nowhere, did I tell you that? They can scream as loud as they like, no one but sheep to hear them."

When we did get up, it was after two in the afternoon. She didn't take me upstairs, but she made a couple of trips for more wine and food. The effects of the fight eventually left her, fell way; she was in a peaceful and graceful mood, her eyes heavily lidded, a look of calm. I told her a little bit about my mother; she listened without reciprocating with any stories of her own. I could tell she wanted to listen, but was still too shattered by the event of the fight to want to offer up anything more of herself for the time being.

The rest of the weekend continued to become more wordless and more strange, the room becoming littered with baguette crusts, orange peels, wine bottles, and other debris and discards.

We managed to easily overcome our stings and aches and continued our lovemaking, turning it into a feral, greedy, and violent act, all over the floor of her flat, wordless and insatiable until we slept, and sleep we did deeply, well into the afternoon hours of Sunday. When I awoke, she was naked, straddling me and looking down on me with a child's intensity; slowly, we started again, the urge made strong by hunger I felt, and the after effects of the wine and hash. Late on Sunday night, we shared another bath and smoked a joint and talked in small voices about the future, our future, and how there wasn't anyone else.

7 · LOVE IN A VOID

I woke with a start on Monday morning, Ailsa asleep beside me. I couldn't see her, so dark was the room, but her warm presence and quiet breathing was electric beside me. Of course, I wanted to take her tenderly and wake her by making love, but I felt a mild panic knowing that I needed to go to work. I needed to catch up with the other life, dig out a clean shirt, some socks, and I wanted to tell Ali everything.

I rose and snuck up the spiral staircase to the kitchen, being very careful to listen out for any parents; but as of late last night, they had not returned from the cottage. It was more likely, Ailsa had said, that they would stay overnight and return early afternoon on the Monday.

The clock on the kitchen wall told me it was eight o'clock. It was light out, pearly white, but not raining. I snuck back down the stairs and dressed, brushed my teeth, and left quietly without waking Ailsa.

I walked past the Torphichen Street police station and then along Morrison Street to Tollcross, where I caught a 16 bus. The high clouds were a dense silver coating on the sky—heavenly, still and mildly threatening.

The weekend hung like a huge exclamation mark in the air. I kept closing my eyes so I could look at Ailsa's face again, recapture her space, her scent, which was heavy and thick on me. I said her name quietly to myself. "Ailsa," and again, "Ailsa," until I said it over and over and over again.

My little daydream of recreating Ailsa took me almost to the end of my street. I pulled out a cigarette and lit it, leapt quickly down the steps from the top deck of the bus, and jumped off at the end of my street. The street was quiet. It was always dead quiet. I got to the flat and wanted to throw some clothes into a bag and turn around back to Ailsa's. Hers was a sanctuary, save for the uneasy feeling I had about her fighting parents, and although this weekend had seen an absolute manifestation of her physical love of me and mine of her, she was still an enigma, she was still an intellectual unknown. However, I could barely let her enter my mind without wanting her entirely again and again. Although I was so gorged full of her, I had a greed and a thirst and I wanted her again.

My bedroom was eerily spotless. Mother had been in to clean, and probably to search as well, looking for evidence of a deviant life to hold aloft as a threat.

There was a note on my bed, squarely in the middle of the stretched-flat bed spread, written on light blue Basildon-bond letter paper. It read, "Wash dishes, dry and put away, hang wet clothing from machine in back garden." This was typical of my mother, hardly surprising, and I went into the kitchen to wash the dishes. It was ten o'clock and I ran the water until it was hot and filled the basin. There were four dishes to wash and as I squeezed the washing up liquid into the basin, I heard a key in the lock. "Fuck," I whispered.

"Showing up exactly when you please, think this place is a bloody hotel. Where have you been?" She filled the doorway of the kitchen, a long belted raincoat on and a mask of betrayal and expectancy wiped all over her face.

"I've been with a friend. Mind your own business, I'm staying out of your way," I said calmly.

"Must be nice to do what you like, is it?"

"Leave me alone, Mum. I'm washing the dishes, then I'll hang out the washing, then I'll go to work."

"And what about your job interview? Pack of bloody lies, wasn't it? I called up and they said there weren't any positions available and to try back later!"

"Mind your own business."

I wiped my hands and walked to the kitchen door.

"You have done NOTHING but waste your time since the day you were born. You did nothing at school, and you're doing nothing now!" she shouted.

"And you're just a miserable old cow!" I shouted back, to which she made an incoherent sound and lunged towards the sink, picked up the still full basin with both hands and threw it hard across the kitchen at me, sending a tidal wave of dishwater, cups, and cutlery scattering all over the kitchen floor.

I gasped, soaked, and started laughing; pure release, as the act of violence and rage played over and over again in my mind. I looked at my mother, one side of her beige raincoat soaked, her face purple with anger as she breathed quickly and deeply, making a wheezing sound. For some reason I just started imitating her breathing back at her, mocking her. "You should be locked up, you mental COW!" I screamed at her. "You're fucking insane!"

"I am not INSANE," she screamed. Her voice now resembled a child's; it was terrifying, and I became terrified about what I might do to her. I left the kitchen and went into my bedroom, locking the door behind me. I stood with my back to the door and listened as I heard her screaming at me and throwing things, culminating in her pulling the telephone from its wire in the wall and smashing it on the floor, the bell ringing once and heralding a silence.

I quickly pulled out a hold-all and filled it with clothes. My mind had been made up for me: *enfants terrible*! I was shaken and couldn't think of what to take. I decided that my books and records were going to be thrown out and to get used to the fact—just get out while you can.

I had a sour metallic taste in my mouth which seemed to be getting stronger. I lit a cigarette and I couldn't hear anything, nothing. As I opened my door silently and slowly tiptoed to the bathroom to get my toothbrush, I realized my keys were on the kitchen table. I would either have to go in there to get them, or just give up and rely on the future. I decided it would be in my best interests to have my keys—insurance or something—but getting them would be like walking past a sleeping dragon.

I put the hold-all with my clothes by the front door, and turned quickly and walked into the kitchen. She had opened the wall-mounted cupboard that housed the tinned and jarred foods and she'd thrown much of it against the wall. Not much had broken save for a jar of beetroot, which left a violent and long streak of purple on the wall, drip marks descending to the kitchen floor, forming a dark pool of purple vinegar, a weeping acidic wound. What a masterstroke, what a deliberate, grand finale.

She was sitting at the kitchen table, shaking. "Don't you ever set foot in this house again," she said, her voice strangled and childlike.

"I won't be back," I said, snatching up my keys.

"Then leave... those... keys," she said through gritted teeth, slowly.

I walked away quickly and grabbed my bag at the front door, leaving to the sound of her screaming "Leave those keys!" at ear-splitting volume from the kitchen.

Much shaken, I walked down the length of the street to Morningside Road. It was a relief to see it fairly busy: multitudes of old-age pensioners and a fair smattering of well-to-do upper-middle-class people mixed with a generous helping of the insane, thanks to the day release programme of the Royal Ed. They'd wander the local streets and parks. Or sit in Morningside Library. We at the supermarket, of course, got our fair share; often they'd come in and knock back huge bottles of cider in the quieter aisles when no one was looking.

Morningside walked on, busy and oblivious to the huge fight that just happened. What would Ailsa think? Would she shy away? Was the fight too similar to the one her mother and stepfather had had on Saturday? The whole thing was such a startling opposite to what had happened over the weekend: the hours of tacit lovemaking, the deep understanding, the adoration dashed on the rocks cruelly like a bird's skull.

Suddenly, I thought I saw her! It was her! A slim, red-headed figure disappearing into Morningside Library. I tore across the street and almost got hit by a postal van. I burst through the wooden double doors of the library, my feverish, frenzied excitement pouring into the thick, warm silence of the library. Old age pensioners reading the papers for free. A few parents with very small children milling about. Ailsa! Looking in one of the fiction aisles. I started towards her and tripped in my haste over an old man's walking stick that protruded from the back of his chair. "Ailsa!" I shouted as I fell, and everyone, including her, turned, shocked at the loud noise.

Thin-lipped with a bird-like face and glasses; at least ten, maybe fifteen years older than she. "I'm sorry, I made a mistake," I said, and got up. "Ye should look where ye'r going son, this is a library, ye cannae run or shout!" the angry owner of the walking stick hissed at me. I looked at him absently, and continued to stare at the older redhead, wishing she would turn into Ailsa. Now I had a real appetite for her, to encircle her with my arms and legs all morning and all day, I could just leave and get on the bus. Leave and get on the bus. Leave and get on the bus.

What now? I could leave my bag in the changing room at work, there was even a shower, so I walked up the road to the supermarket and went straight to the staff room.

"How's the airm, big guy?" It was Rory Campbell from the liquor department sitting at a table reading a tabloid and smoking. He was a portly, affable fellow, far smarter than he let on.

"Well, you know what they say about wanker's cramp, Rory," I said, beating him to the inevitable punch. "It's fine now though, thanks." I lit a cigarette and helped myself to a coffee in a polystyrene cup from a huge silver urn and sat down at one of the long white Formica-topped tables.

There were a few people dotted about the canteen. A couple of overnight drivers, exhausted and hunched over coffee and bacon rolls, another couple of night crew, whiling away time until the Merlin opened across the street.

The room was large and wholly functional, a countertop and kitchen at one end, where, for about thirty pence, you could enjoy a three-course meal at lunchtime. The standards were that of school or hospital dinners, served by Macbeth's three witches.

Jess Watson shuffled in and I gathered my nerves. She chain-smoked and looked sixty, although she was probably in her early forties. She looked at me. "Ye'll no be needing a doctor's line then," she stated rather than asked.

"NO Jess, I'm fine, it feels a lot better."

"All right then, son."

She poured a cup of coffee and picked up a bacon roll from a tray on the counter, putting a ten pence piece in an empty coffee tin. She sat down and lit a cigarette, taking a bite out of the roll at the same time as inhaling the first smoke. It was a topic of conversation between me and Ali that she would stop smoking for nothing. She smoked through every meal, she didn't even know she was doing it, stopping only to let out a hacking cough.

"Do you need anyone just now, Jess? I'm not on until this afternoon," I asked.

"Well, you could go and help them unload a lorry in the back, they're doing it just now."

I got up and went through to the changing room and put on my uniform, grateful for some physical labour to do. The fight with my mother was still too present in my mind and I was starting to feel the pining pangs of missing Ailsa— she had not wanted me to leave, the night before; she had made me promise I would come back after work. I told her I would, after I had talked to Ali, maybe eleven or twelve. It seemed like days away. At the back door, a huge truck was being emptied and just as I started in with the other men there, a wave of exhaustion hit me and I felt sluggish and drained. There was a very real temptation to walk away and just go to Ailsa's now and start everything again, take her up on the offer of a roof over my head, free rent, anonymity, and sex; to lie in the clandestine still-life of her room. Maybe she was there right now, sitting in the peace, drawing a feathered charcoal sky on the deep cream of her paper.

"There he is, the invisible man, all right there?" It was Ali. "Where've ye been?"

"Sprained my wrist," I said with an astute wink.

"Oh, aye, right enough," he said.

"Aye, I was told to convalesce for a few days, doctor's orders," I smiled.

"Is it too sprained tae pick up a pint glass?" Ali asked, mock concern in his voice.

"Oh, I think I can manage that."

"Canny Man's the night, then, and no the Merlin, I'm fuckin' sick of they heedcases," Ali raised his voice slightly at the end of the sentence, implicating the people working around us, garnering an immediate chorus of "Shut up ya wee poof" and "Away and drink yer babycham, ya cunt." All seemed approaching normal again and I felt a bit better.

"Oh, by the way, big man, your ma's out there shopping, I'm away tae have ma lunch before I start," and he left.

I froze. This had happened before, after a fight and before work. She had shown up at work with considerable remorse and managed to embarrass me in front of everyone by crying at my checkout. Please go away, please go away, please go away.

All of a sudden, the tannoy system burst into life. "Adam Kelvin, aiphone please, Adam Kelvin." It was Jess's voice. The aiphone was a two way telephone that connected you from anywhere in the store to either Jess's office or the manager's office. Being called to the aiphone was usually never a good thing. I picked up the white plastic receiver.

"Hello, Jess."

"Right Adam, take over on checkout seven from Cheryl, she's away home not well. Come and get a drawer from me now," she said, and hung up. Timing. Now I was a sitting duck for my mother's unpredictable temper. I walked to the office using the circumference of the store rather than cutting quickly across it. The office was up a short flight of steps and the door was always locked with a plexiglass window complete with a slot large enough to allow the passage back and forth of cash register drawers.

"There ye go, son," said Jess, and passed out a drawer to me. "Number seven." The drawers were counted before and after each shift. There was no allowance for overage or underage, to the penny it had to be, or questions were asked.

I walked down the stairs and to checkout seven, put the drawer in and closed it, and activated the cash register with my key; two quick beeps and it came alive.

"Are you open?" a demanding upper-middle-class voice, whining behind a huge trolley piled high with groceries.

"Open for business!" I chirped cheerily as sausages, tinfoil, marmalade, and fruit started to rain onto the conveyor belt. As with the rest of Morningside, the clientele was diverse and often very well-to-do. Many were ancient relics, pre-dating even World War I; permanently confused by progress, bewildered by the bright convenience of the supermarket, and terrified of being overcharged.

There was also a small and dedicated circle of my friends who would come in and load up their grocery trolleys with wine and beer, with a smattering of actual groceries on top. They would come to my checkout and I would ring up only the groceries—a loaf of bread, a couple of tins, some milk—and mime my way through ringing up the rest of the sale, thus enabling the friend to pay perhaps a pound or two for a weekend's worth of drink. This could only happen at very select times. The "shopping" friend would come into the store and walk nearby my checkout. I would give a very discreet nod if everything was okay, a quick shake of the head would let it be known that this was not a good time.

I was in the middle of ringing up some highly-strung woman when one such friend entered the store, his apparent breeziness offset considerably by his face, which was focused and scrutinizing, kind of how I imagined a safecracker at work might look. I smiled to myself. Colin McQueen was a couple of years older than I was and lived very nearby with three other guys in a flat. This was where I bought my hash and was the scene of many long nights smoking joints, bongs, chillums, pipes and listening to incredible music from Africa and Arabia and strange jazz, made stranger by smoking. He was an affable guy and always welcomed me and my friends into his flat. He also didn't abuse the free alcohol offer I had made. I gave him the nod as he walked past, and he turned away to continue his shopping.

A few minutes later, I had built up a bit of a queue and I didn't notice him join it. My eyes were down looking at the chocolate digestives, tins of beans, toothpaste and laundry detergents as they whizzed by, my left hand pulling them past me into the bagging area, my right hand punching the numeric keys on the cash register. Eventually, I saw his head peering out of the queue, two people back. "Hello there! What're ye up to?" I asked him, smiling.

"Och, nothing much, you know, the usual game plan for the unemployed."

I finished ringing up the two customers in front of him, and then rang up his chocolate biscuits and a loaf of bread. I pulled two bottles of Valpolicello across and pretended to ring them up, then pretended to ring up four cans of Kestrel lager. Colin bent forward a little and spoke in a low voice. "Eh, your ma's standing right behind you, do you know that?" he asked.

I turned around and, sure enough, there she was, standing stalk still and staring at me, still wearing the beige raincoat with the huge water stain on it, her bottom lip curled slightly down revealing a portion of her teeth. She looked like a cornered dog. I could not be anything except polite to her. I was in my work clothes, Colin was here. The last thing I wanted was the scene I knew she was more than capable of creating. "Hello, there, Mum! And what can I do for you?" I asked brightly, smiling.

She leaned forward and I was hit with a wave of fear as I braced myself for what she might say. "I'll wait a minute until you are not busy," was what she said, with the enunciation of a schoolteacher reading to a five-year-old.

I charged Colin the fifty pence or whatever it was and he gave me an appreciative smile. "Thanks, Adam, come by for a wee smoke up after work if ye want," he said quietly and left.

I rang up the next customer, feeling like I was living on borrowed time, the huge presence of my mother burning a hole in me from behind. There then came a lull in customers and I turned to her. She came forward, just a little slowly, as if she was walking onstage.

"What would you like for your tea tonight?" she asked in a quavering voice.

"I'm not coming home, Mum, and you really shouldn't come into my work like this," I replied.

"Shall I get one of these pizzas from the refrigerated section?" she quavered again, a little more hysteria. I knew it was close to breaking point, whatever it was.

"I think you should just leave me alone."

She drew back and stared at me for a good long five seconds, then turned and left. Thank god, I thought, it could have been full-on hysterics. But then, as I started ringing up the next customer, she was there again at the back of the checkout. She leaned in and spoke in a grating, hoarse-sounding voice. "I saw what you did with that drug dealer a minute ago," letting the phrase 'drug dealer' rise above the other words as if throwing it in the air for all to see. She turned and walked away quickly.

I didn't know what it meant exactly, was she about to report me? Had she guessed what I was doing? Although anyone close who had seen the small handful of coins Colin had given me would know that it was an inadequate sum to cover what he had actually walked out with. My mother was in predator mode.

She wanted something and was going to messily smash down everything in her way to get it, whatever 'it' was.

My mother had quickly put two and two together regarding Colin's selling hash; she also connected any drug with chronic heroin addiction. She could tell when I was stoned and had recently staged an intervention on my behalf. I had risen one morning to find her in the living room with a wizened and desperate-looking man smoking a rolled-up cigarette. This was an ex-junkie, and my mother told me to "listen to what he had to offer me" in her nursery school teacher voice, at which point she left. I patiently listened to the shell of a man drone on and on about "how cool it wiz tae get high" and "how fuckin' amazin' it wiz tae stick a needle in yer airm" and how "it wisnae long until yer stealing frae yer own ma." I told him thanks, but I had never used heroin, or any other drug for that matter, except hash and alcohol, and was not likely to.

"Aye, well yer ma thinks different, son." He looked up at me with watery eyes and a cloying smile.

"Yes, well, my ma thinks the upstairs neighbours moved in specifically to persecute her, and they are four quiet Napier students. She also painted graffiti on my bedroom wall when she was pissed off at me for something, and she drinks too much and takes Valium, okay?" I had become angry.

"Let me see your airms," he asked, adding an unnecessary "please."

I rolled up my sleeves, displaying milky white, untainted flesh. "Ye can help yourself tae any of the precious ornaments ye see in here, silver cutlery's in the kitchen. I'm leaving, ya junkie bastard," and with that I got up and walked out.

"Ye don't have tae listen tae it, Adam, you're the one in control..." but I was gone.

I called Ali over to my checkout, still afraid of what my mother was going to do and wanting some down-to-earth camaraderie. "I just gave McQueen a bathful of red wine, we could go over to his after if ye want, have a bit of a smoke."

Ali's grin spread from ear to ear. "Aye, that'd be fuckin' brilliant. I could do with a smoke, I'm totally out maself," and he peeled back to wherever he had been working before. Eventually, as the earlier violence of my mother stopped shaking me, my mind, naturally, returned to Ailsa. I thought again about her parents in the stark early-morning sun, against the relief of the sandy coloured buildings, doing a strange dance of sudden movements, their voices like bullwhips, cracking across the day, shrieking and snapping.

I thought about Ailsa and her head on my chest, at peace. About how I could give her peace and miracles every single day, and the sanctuary of her flat, white wine and beautiful green pears, the sun seen through the blue-green glass of the phrenology head, the adventurous but subdued sonatas of the water of Leith.

"Break, Adam." I was being relieved for fifteen minutes. I was glad, I needed a cigarette, though it felt far too early for my first break. The woman relieving me was squat and fat with an impassive face underneath poorly bleached hair. "Jess wants to see ye in the office, don't be late back," she said, and settled into my seat, giving me my cash drawer which I covered and locked. This was mandatory every time you came or went to your position: take your drawer, cover it and lock it. Such is the paranoia of large scale commerce, I suppose.

I walked up the stairs and passed the drawer to Jess through the office door window. "Thank you, Adam" she said, and put it down behind her. She then opened the door, which surprised me. "We're going to Mr. Chamber's office." Mr Chambers was the manager, a man I had never had real reason to speak to, and he was happy, seemingly, not to speak to me, or any of my co-workers. A neatly attired, bland-looking man in his mid forties, his office boasted a wall that was a huge one-way mirror that looked out over the store, with a grandstand view of every checkout.

As we entered his office, I developed a sick feeling in the pit of my stomach. But how could he know? Even with the most powerful hunting binoculars, it would be impossible for him to see what I was ringing up as far away as checkout seven. Was it to do with my sprained wrist story? Were there holes in that story?

He turned from looking out the one-way mirror and looked at me. "Right, Adam, now I have no way of proving this at the moment and I am very reluctant to spend the time and resources to do so—because it would mean a complete stock check of the liquor department to be done after we close this evening—but I have it on very good authority that someone passed through your checkout this morning without paying for several bottles of wine." He stopped and looked at me with a hard stare. How are you expected to start speaking after hearing something like that? It was like being beaten up really quickly and really efficiently; it took your breath away, I searched my entire being for a way to speak and I could feel my mouth move slowly, like a fish out of water.

"Do... you... mean someone shoplifted them and made off with them through my checkout? I didn't see anything, if that's what you're asking. I'm sorry, I don't remember anything unusual..." I couldn't have sounded any more pathetic, my voice a whining child's, my face hot and wet.

Chambers lost his clipped professional tone quickly. "Aye, maybe you don't remember because the person who I believe you helped take them is a fucking druggy and a friend of yours."

"Well, yes, I rang up a friend of mine today, but..."

"Right then, listen: I would like very much to press criminal charges on the pair of yous, but I don't want tae pay the fuckin' overtime to have the stock check done, so you can leave now and don't set foot in here again, understood?"

I was gearing up to fight and hang onto the lie like a log in an angry river, but all of a sudden, I saw and felt Ailsa in my mind and realized that I didn't have to. I could walk away, she was there for me with open arms, it was what she wanted, and now, my mind had been made up for me.

"I just need to get my bag from the changing room."

"See to it he leaves, Jess. Page someone from the backroom to make sure of it," he said tersely.

"I'm going, don't worry, I just need my bag," I said dully.

"What's in the bag, Adam?" he asked, heavy sarcasm in his voice.

"Clothes, a change of clothes, nothing from here," I replied.

"All right, then I'll accompany you to the changing room and have a check myself, if you don't mind."

He got up from his desk and we left his office, walking down the flight of stairs and onto the shop floor. My face felt sunburned, it was so red. Why didn't he just ask me to take my clothes off in front of the entire store? I immediately saw Ali; from his face I could tell that he knew I had been caught: shock, fear, and genuine sympathy.

We walked up the public stairs that led to the car park, the canteen, and the changing rooms.

Once inside the changing room, I retrieved the bag from my locker and unzipped it. I was worried that my tobacco tin, which contained a little hash and Rizla papers, was on top, but it wasn't, just the clothes I had hastily thrown in earlier that day, as I had said to Chambers. "Right, you can leave now," he said, sighing, and I got up and walked quickly down the stairs and out onto Morningside Road.

I thought about going straight to Ailsa's, but was worried about showing up unannounced. What would I do if she weren't home? Sit outside and wait? What if I got there and the parents were screaming again? Dragons guarding the castle gates.

I didn't know enough about her to know any of her patterns. I know she didn't have a job. Everything she said seemed to indicate that she had no plans other than the occasional charcoal drawing, lying around drinking wine, and fucking me. Cash seemed to be no object. I really hoped she had no plans.

I decided to visit Colin. I was pretty certain he was home and knew he would have plenty of sympathy. He lived in the top flat of a tenement at the end of Maxwell Street, a short street south of the supermarket that backed onto a small railway yard. I climbed the stairs and knocked on his door.

"Who is it?" Colin asked.

"It's me, Adam," I replied.

He opened the door smiling, "Lunch break, aye?"

"No... I got fired."

"Fuck, not because of me, was it?" He looked shocked.

I sighed. "No, no, I think my mum put two and two together when she seen you at the checkout—mind she was standing behind us? Well, she's pretty mental, she went mad at me this morning, threw a jar of beetroot at the wall, came into the shop to try and pretend it hadn't happened. I told her I wasn't coming home, basically..." I stopped talking.

There was a pause.

"Come on in. I'm really sorry, man, what're ye going to do?" he asked.

"Och, I hated that dump. You know I did, fuck it."

"Let's have a wee smoke then."

We relaxed and he put on one of my favourite records: "Charm" by Brian Eno and John Hassell, a long melancholic loop of lazy percussion and synthesizer with a mad serpentine trumpet on top.

I told him a bit about Ailsa and what she'd said about looking after me, how she had encouraged me to quit anyway, and how I would spend the rest of my life in her West End basement, eating her parents' food and having sex.

"Careful though, man, it sounds brilliant, but her mum and dad sound pretty mental."

"Oh, and my mum doesn't? I can deal with the mad parents."

"Right, but what if she, or they, throw you out? What'll ye do then?" he asked.

"I'll just come here," I laughed.

8 · THE STAIRCASE MYSTERY

The afternoon wore on and we walked down to Morningside Cemetery, taking with us a bottle of the stolen wine, where we passed it between each other and talked more. Eventually, a little drunk and stoned, with the afternoon sun wan in the sky, I decided to head for Ailsa's. Colin and I walked out of the cemetery, back to his street. The beginning of dusk and the presence of the scent of cut grass and flowers gave the afternoon a magical feel. We joked that we wouldn't be surprised if we saw some dancing fairies in the grass.

I boarded a number 16 bus after saying my goodbyes to Colin, with the promise of getting together for another smoke soon. I began to worry about my situation whilst sitting on the bus, my hold-all on my knees, the only thing in the world I had at this point. What would I do for money? And what if Ailsa threw me out? This continued to nag and worry me as I got off the bus at the West End and walked down Shandwick Place, eventually ending up at her door.

She was delighted to see me and pulled me in, kissing me hard immediately. "You're early, I'm so happy!" she said and jumped up, wrapping her legs around my waist. She was, of course, far more beautiful than my memory had allowed me to think. "I've been drawing a picture of you, come and look," she said, getting off me. Taking my hand, she led me over to the bed, on which there was a pad of paper, my likeness in 2B pencil sketched on top. It was really accurate.

"Drawn from memory," she said.

"It's remarkable. God, you're very good, Ailsa," a tingle as I said her name.

"How did you get to leave so early?" she asked, pulling me down to sit on the bed.

"Fired. I was fired. I was giving away wine to the populace."

She laughed. "Who'd you give it to? A free bottle to every customer?"

"No," I sighed. "My friend, Colin, he's on the dole. I sort him out when he comes in."

"Then I am very grateful to Colin because now I have you all to myself." She turned to face me on the bed and climbed on my lap, putting her arms around my shoulders.

"Yep, you do, I even brought some stuff from home, some clothes. I hope the offer is still open, my mother kind of threw me out today as well," I said resignedly.

"Of course it is, how could it not be? No way, it couldn't be." She kissed me.

"I really need to earn though, I have to find some kind of job, I..."

"You're hired, you can work for me. You want to earn something?" She kissed me again. I was not sure exactly what she was getting at. "You want some money? Then help yourself." She kissed me again. "Here's how. My stepfather keeps cash in a manila envelope in his office." Her voice became lower and more seductive. She punctuated her speech with kisses and slowly moved on my lap. "It's in his desk, top drawer on the right. It's always on the top, it's the first thing you'll see. It won't be locked, he doesn't care, I've been helping myself for years. I know he must know, but he doesn't care—and we could do with some pocket money so why don't you go up and get some? Go up the stairs to the very top floor. His office is facing you, it's the only one with a frosted glass door, it's never locked."

I could tell she was perfectly serious, and that this had nothing to do with the money.

"Can't you just ask him?" I asked lamely.

"And where's the fun in that, Adam? I'll tell you what. You do this thing for me, and I'll give you a very special treat when you come back."

I was still giddy from the wine, still stoned, and my paranoia started to stir.

"But even if I was just walking up there, if either of them saw me—they don't know who I am, they'll just think I'm a burglar," I reasoned.

"Well, you are," she laughed. "No, then you just tell them you're Ailsa's boyfriend. You were sent up to get a bottle of wine from the wine closet and you can't find it, okay? You are my boyfriend, Adam, aren't you?" She pulled me tightly to her.

"Yes, of course."

She got off me and my heart started to pound. I was actually going to do this. My mouth was going dry, and I felt my face, for the third or fourth time that day, go deep red, a pounding red heat, and the early promise of a brutal headache.

"Where are they just now?" I asked.

"Watching telly, most likely, upstairs." She gave a barely noticeable sigh of exasperation. "There's no way either of them will go upstairs to the top floor unless they absolutely have to, their bedroom is the floor below. If they fight now, all the better, one of them will leave the house and the other will sit and get drunk and most likely fall asleep in front of the telly. Don't worry, Adam, you're perfectly safe."

I had no choice. What was the worst thing that could happen? If I came face to face with one of them, I could say that Ailsa asked me to do it. Or I could just run as quickly as I could and never come back.

She gave a smile that was at once sweetly victorious and a little sympathetic as I sighed and got up, walking to the spiral staircase and ascending it. I had not been upstairs into the main house before, just the kitchen, and that only fleetingly, so I had no idea as to the layout of the house other than the parts Ailsa had described. All I knew is that I needed to find the staircase and keep walking up until I could not walk up any more. If I happened to encounter either of her parents on the ground floor, I could easily bluff my way through with charm and honest bewilderment. But a wine cupboard? Who in the world keeps a wine cupboard next to a bedroom? Or, more ridiculous still, on the top floor, as far away from the dining room as possible?

I walked up the spiral staircase from Ailsa's basement in semi-darkness as the summer evening continued to descend on everything. There was still plenty of light in the kitchen as I entered. There was huge island in the middle of the floor, a surface for slicing and preparing. Above it, hanging from the ceiling, were all manner of pots and pans, copper and otherwise. There was a huge double sink underneath the window which looked out onto the long, narrow garden. The fading light gave the impression that everything outside was monochrome. There was a square table and chairs in the corner and a huge refrigerator.

Opening the kitchen door, I walked out into the lobby. I could see the front door, it was flanked by two long glass panels that stretched its entire length to the floor. There were two other doors, but they were closed. One of these doors must be separating me from the parents. I could not hear any television; I was hoping that there would be something to mask the sound I was making. I strained—nothing. Were they sitting in utter silence? Staring at each other?

I looked at the staircase I had to ascend: wide brown stairs mercifully carpeted to hide the sound of my feet on what was probably very creaky wood. The lobby also boasted an amazingly ornate, sculpted dark wooden table with a huge vase of flowers making a tasteful plume in the dim area. The lobby smelled of expensive polish and the soft fragrance of the bouquet in the vase. Much of the floor area was occupied by a beautiful rug of scarlet and muted gold.

The stairs responded to my feet with a low whine that I am sure my terrified mind amplified tenfold as I began to steadily ascend.

The house was huge, tall as a small city tenement building. I am sure I have mentioned this, but I could not believe the size. The doors on the first and second floors were all shut, and with each step I waited, tensed, for one of them to burst open and to be attacked by one of the two people I had seen screaming on the street a couple of days ago. The silence was almost absolute. Could I hear the muted tick-tock of a grandfather clock? No hushed conversation, no cutlery on plates. I begged for another screaming argument, because then I would know where the enemy was situated. The reluctant bend of the wooden stairs, its sound quietly seeping out to the rest of the house; I tried to lessen each creak by resolving to make the next footstep lighter than the last but there was no difference, it was like the sound of a wooden giant lightly snoring. I imagined it ricocheting off all the Georgian walls of the New Town.

Eventually I had made my way to the top and, sure enough, there was the office door, closed, made of frosted glass panels. I gently pushed the door handle down. It gave easily and I was in.

I went straight for the desk which faced the left wall. There was plenty of light allowed in by a huge window. I pulled open the drawer and saw an envelope that fit Ailsa's description. I opened it: hundreds of pounds, at least four or five hundred in twenties. Who kept that kind of cash on hand? I stuck my hand in and counted off four. In my controlled panic, four seemed to not be as alarming or devastating as five, which would have been a round hundred. I thought I was somehow being humble by only helping myself to eighty.

I folded them and put them in my back pocket, closing the drawer slowly and carefully. Now that the crime was committed, I felt like I had the luxury of being more attentive to my surroundings. This, of course, was ridiculous; I could still be caught red handed. I was a thief in a stranger's house and would remain at risk until I was back downstairs with Ailsa.

I closed the office door quietly, keeping the door-handle down until I knew the latch could engage soundlessly. I padded down the stairs as quietly as I could; again, each step was more excruciating than the last as I kept waiting for doors to burst open, voices to ring out accusingly, but each step took me closer to the safety of the basement. I entered the kitchen and sharply drew in my breath as I saw a figure bent down in front of an open cupboard. My eyes widened for a fraction of a second and my heart slammed against my ribs, but it was Ailsa. She turned round casually. "Supplies," she said airily and pulled out two bottles of red wine. "And now for your surprise, angel. Come on."

I followed her downstairs, distracted and nervous, but the relief from having completed my task loosened my muscles, cleared my sinuses. I was high with the feeling.

This feeling continued to escalate as Ailsa put down the wine, sat me on the bed and unzipped my trousers, pulling out my cock and letting her tongue playfully work around it as I grew and grew. This had never been done to me before and the fast beating of my heart from stealing the money turned into the fast beating of my heart from her lips around me, her soft hands holding me. My release spread an unthinkable serenity through my whole being. The sound of a solo cello playing cast its somber wooden shadow throughout the room, the melancholy key bringing a touch of glorious autumn into the midsummer night.

I had my answer. Why, why would I do this? Why did I climb the stairs in silence, in a stranger's house? Why did I steal, simply because I was asked to? The answer was in the toilet rinsing her mouth out, the answer walked back into the living room and looked at me whilst pushing back her tousled red hair from her eyes. I felt like my ribs were being torn from my body to reveal a sick, fat heart which beat too fast. Did I live here now? With the answer? Would the answer have me? I would do anything, anything, for the answer.

"How much, then?" she asked.

"Huh? Oh, uh, sixty quid, I think" I answered absently.

"Nice one, hand it over," she smiled, holding out her hand and rubbing her thumb quickly against her middle finger.

I reached into my pocket and gave her three of the four folded twenty-pound notes, then picked up my cigarettes. I offered her one, and lighting my own, right at that moment, the phone in her room rang. It gave us both a start. The ring was loud and modern sounding, a high pitched flutter coming from her side of the bed. She answered it.

"Hello?" She stood listening to the other end while letting her eyes wander around the room. "Okay, yeah, well I'll see you when you get back, yeah? Bye." As she put the phone down smiling wryly to herself, she turned to me. "Mum and my stepdad won't be back until tomorrow night."

Incomprehension, then incredulity swept like storms across my face. She looked at me and sniggered, her eyes mischievous and kind at the same time.

"Had to see if you had the balls, and lo and behold, you have the balls!" she laughed.

"I was fucking crapping myself the whole time!" I said, truly astonished.

"Well, you didn't show it, you were marvellous! A simulated test environment." She bent down and kissed me on the lips. "And we have sixty quid to play with!"

"I wondered why there wasn't even a single sound, no TV, no newspapers rustling! Fuck me, I can't believe it!" I marvelled.

"Sixty quid and a blowjob. Not bad for a night's work, yeah?" she laughed.

"Come on, I'll take you on a proper tour of the house, if you want." She took my hand and we walked up the spiral staircase and into the kitchen. "You live here now, angel, you can come up anytime you like and help yourself to anything. They won't care, I promise—they'll be glad, they won't have to worry about me being alone when they scrap." She pointed to the fridge. "Fridge, in case you didn't know." She turned and pointed to a wall-mounted cabinet. "Tea, coffee, sugar, biscuits," then she walked over to the cupboard I had seen her crouched at when I had come down from stealing the money. "Wine, wine, wine," she deadpanned as she opened the door. "If you want anything stronger it's in the living room across the hall—whiskey, vodka, gin, mixers, all there."

I followed her into the lobby and she turned the light on. I had not noticed before, but there was a painting on the wall of a red-haired little girl. The whole painting was pretty dark; with the red hair stark against the black background, it had a somewhat Victorian appearance.

"How old were you when your mum did that?" I asked.

"Bingo! Clever clogs! I was four, such a fucking brat, I was, too," she said.

"It's really good, it's a really good painting."

"Oh, she's good, she sells quite a bit, or has sold quite a bit. I don't know if she's sold anything recently, but she's supposed to be held in pretty high regard in that world."

I looked around me and up the stairs. I knew the place was enormous, but with the lights on, it was this timeless, endless, palatial expanse. Without any of the other doors open, the only thing that betrayed its late-20th-century placement was the telephone on the hall table. Perhaps it was the mixture of the darkness, the muted and luxurious pigments of many of the objects, and Ailsa's portrait that gave it a 19th-century ambience and veneer.

The living room boasted a huge fireplace complete with black marble mantle. There were a few paintings, some small sculptures, and tasteful trinkets revealing that the exact placement in time was now, and that whomever had decorated (I assumed Ailsa's mother) had impeccable taste. Bohemian, but very understated and with a sense of space. Unless I was way off the mark, the stepfather had little say or interest in the surroundings.

As I looked around, I could see that Ailsa was disinterested also, but in the way that someone who grows up in a castle doesn't care that they grew up in a castle. It's only when someone visits and gapes in awe at the grandeur that the fact of their domicile is shown up in such stark relief.

"Wait here a second," she said, and noticed the briefest of alarmed expressions on my face. "Don't worry, a mad dog's not going to jump in and eat you," and she sprinted downstairs, returning less than a minute later with a joint, a blanket, and a bottle of wine. "The roof," she said, "stars, planets," and she took my hand and we walked up the stairs with no heed to the creak of the wood that had provided the soundtrack to my absolute fear so recently. "There are so many fucking rooms in this place. I think Mum and my stepdad had wanted more kids—in fact, I know they did, not just mopey old me—but it never happened. They'll probably offer you a whole floor if you want it, unless Dad finds out you've been stealing from him," she laughed with the merest hint of malice, but I was sure I made that up.

On the top floor, she went into her stepfather's office. Now it was just an office, benign, un-booby-trapped. She opened up a cupboard door by the window and pulled out a set of stepladders. The cupboard was crammed with fishing equipment and hunting gear. "It's all my mum'll let him have for his outdoorsy stuff." She passed me the ladders and motioned to the door. At the top of the stairs there was a trapdoor in the ceiling. She scaled the ladder and pushed open the hatch, climbing in, I followed. The attic was huge and dim. She had pulled on a single bulb on a slim chain, but it only cast light so far, making the farthest reaches of the attic impossible to see, so shrouded in darkness they were. You could hear the staggered dripping of the water tank, and without seeing it, it gave the attic space an impossible ambience at odds with the close dry woodiness of our surroundings. "Don't step between the beams, whatever you do," said Ailsa. The beams that made up the floor were spaced about a foot apart and packed with fibreglass insulation. She pushed open a small glass skylight and, after putting the wine and blanket out first, pulled herself out. Her moves were stealthy and serpentine. I followed her out.

We were above the city. The roof was not flat; we were nestled on a rectangular strip, maybe ten feet by four feet, between two gables. There were a few cigarette ends and roaches, so I could tell this was a favourite haunt of Ailsa's. She threw the blanket on the roof and sat down, lighting the joint. I remained standing, taking in the view that went clear all the way to Fife. You could see Calton Hill out to Cockenzie Power Station. Every beautiful rooftop in the New Town was visible for the last time that day. Streetlights and the remaining light from the heavens serenaded the city.

Ailsa passed the joint to me. "I came up here just a few nights before I met you and just lay down and stared up. There were all these amazing shooting stars. God, it was the loveliest night."

The air had a rich, underlying warmth. You could smell the earthy sweetness of grass and trees from lazily heating all day; it reminded me of Ailsa's complicated beauty. I passed the joint back.

"I knew I was going to meet you, then, Adam, when all these shooting stars were coming down. I thought, one of them is my angel and the rest can burn up in the atmosphere, just don't burn up my angel."

I took off my shirt, gently pushed her back onto the blanket, extinguished the joint, and removed her shirt. We made love again, a celestial brightness bathed her as I cupped her face in my hands, her closed eyes accentuating thick, dark red eyebrows, stark against soft white skin. I sucked in her bottom lip and fell in love again. It made sense that she'd played with me like a toy, total sense, and I had her now, my arms around her as I thrust hard and came quickly, all the shooting stars she had talked of swirled and fell into me and then into her, becoming a luminous starlit fluid. I was no longer there, I felt like I could stand up and fly off the roof.

"Tell me about your other lovers, my love." We were sitting in the kitchen, smoking cigarettes and drinking wine, a bread board between us on the table with brie, pâté, and some water biscuits.

"I've only really had two other girlfriends," I said. "One called Lucy, when I was fourteen, all a bit awkward really, and then Jackie. We split up last summer but we still get along really well. She's all right."

"She's all right," said Ailsa back, quickly, not a question, not mocking, just a statement. Then spoken loudly, "You love me, don't you Adam? You love this? All of this and you want me, don't you?" she said, the words coming out of her mouth with a seemingly rehearsed rapidity, like she was reading them from a script.

"More than anything, Ailsa, you know that," I said softly.

"Then cut her out, Adam. No more, okay?" She spoke quickly and forcefully, the voice was not the sensual lazy flow I was used to.

I thought about Jackie and I thought about her fondly. I wasn't prepared to not be friends with her—we'd shared so much, it just didn't make any sense. She was troubled, but she was kind and beautiful. But what Ailsa had was so powerful. She carried a strength and charisma that felt like a sugar-coated left hook every time I caught her eye. I sighed and reached across the table, taking her hand. "Look, I can't just cut her out, she's a good, good soul, and she's absolutely no threat to me and you. You'd probably really like her too, I mean, it's been about a year since we stopped going out." My voice had a touch of whininess to it that disgusted me.

I thought I saw Ailsa reaching for the cigarettes or her wine glass in my peripheral vision as I looked at her face, but she picked up the short cheese knife, with its sharply curved blade and two pointed tines, and very quickly and forcefully scratched the length of my forearm whilst her other hand gripped my hand with surprising strength. I didn't feel it at first, so I didn't really know what she'd done. I thought she was playing a joke until I saw the pale red line on my forearm start to ooze blood in large, carbuncular beads. It looked like a crudely made necklace laid out straight. Then the sting came, sure and strong, turning into a sharp pain. My jaw dropped and a sound that was half a laugh, half a gasp came out as my eyes opened as wide as they could. I looked from the wound to Ailsa.

She leaned forward, her face and lips tight and white, her eyes wide and insane-looking.

"Fuck her, Adam. She does not exist, not in our WORLD, is that clear?" The word 'world' was snarled and my heart leapt and started hammering in my chest. The silence that followed was leaden. I could not say anything. I looked into her clear eyes that carried an incredible strength and madness.

Eventually she spoke, with something approaching nonchalance. "There's a bottle of TCP and a first-aid kit in the toilet over there." She cocked her head in the direction of the bathroom that adjoined the kitchen. "Bring it out and I'll clean this up for you."

I got up, dripping blood on the floor, and walked numbly over to the small bathroom. Inside, there was a doorless cupboard with a first-aid kit next to some white hand towels on a shelf. The TCP was sitting on a glass shelf above the toilet along with several other bottles of aspirin and lotions. I turned on the tap on the bathroom sink and tried to wash some of the blood off my arm, which was oozing out quite profusely now. The water stung harshly. I brought the kit out to Ailsa, still feeling numb, and put it on the table. She looked up at me, her eyes filled with tears, looking like a frightened animal rather than the ice-cold sadist of less than two minutes ago.

"I have a horrible temper, Adam, it's horrible. I got it from my mum, I can't help it. I'm so, so sorry. Please let me make it better, let me see the wound, I'm sorry." I sat down and placed my arm on the table in front of her, my tongue thick and dry in my mouth. I wanted to say something, but I just couldn't. She took a small ball of cotton wool and placed it over the neck of the TCP bottle, upending it quickly. She very gingerly dabbed the wound. I smarted and she whispered "I'm so sorry" again. Eventually, she had cleaned it up, and she dressed it and wrapped a bandage around my forearm. I still hadn't said anything. As she slipped a small safety pin through the bandage, securing it, she looked up at me.

"Are you going to leave now? Are you? I don't blame you." Her voice was inflected with childlike fear and more than a little resignation.

"I'm not leaving, just please don't be angry at me, Ailsa, I can't bear it, please." I looked at her seriously. "Besides, I don't have anywhere to go anymore," at which I started laughing, the absolute ludicrousness of the past ten minutes hitting me like a giddy punch.

Ailsa got up and sat on my lap, facing me and put her arms around my neck. "Nowhere else to go," she said in a sing-song voice.

Of course it had not occurred to me to leave, to leave and seek a safety zone—there were no safety zones, this was my safety zone. I had no money, no income, nothing. I was beyond exhausted at this point as well. It had to have been about midnight, really not that late, but the last twelve or so hours had rolled into one timeless drain of my mother, my job, wine in the hot afternoon, stealing, sex, culminating in a vicious flesh wound.

"Ailsa, I have to lie down," I said, picking up my wine glass to take a drink, then thinking the better of it and putting it back down. "I'm so tired, I just have to lie down."

"Of course you do, come on." She took my hand and led me down the stairs to her bed, attacker to nurse, attacker to nurse. I lay down and she lay down beside me. I fell asleep immediately.

I dreamt about Jackie. We were sitting beside each other in a classroom at school, which was in the storeroom in the back of the supermarket. It was dark and wet.

I woke up to the sound of rain hammering the pavement above Ailsa's flat. Water cascading down a drain from a pipe on the wall outside let me know that this was a heavy, heavy rain. Ailsa was sleeping deeply and it was dark from the blackout shutters. I couldn't tell if it was still dark outside and I couldn't see a clock anywhere.

The dream about Jackie had left me melancholy; I wanted to see her. The emotional impact of the last few days hit me and I found myself crying. I could not look to Ailsa for comfort. Her violent outburst the night before had scared and shocked me and I felt like a five-year-old. There was to be no comfort.

I wiped the salty tears from my face and got up, walking carefully to the windows in the blackness. I pushed my eye right up to the gap in the blackouts and I could vaguely tell that there was some kind of light outside.

I felt around on the floor and found a dressing gown. I put it on and made my way carefully up to the kitchen. The sky outside was pewter. I could hear the muffled roar of very distant thunder, maybe over Fife, or over the Forth. The clock in the kitchen read half past five. I wanted to feel elated and exuberant about Ailsa but I couldn't find the feeling that I had before. It was lost somewhere. I had to find it again.

I crept back down to the flat, found my clothes, dressed, and left by the door into the back garden.

It was pouring hard. I was angry at myself for not looking for an umbrella, then I remembered that I had kept behind a twenty pound note for myself. I walked to the end of the street—no reason to run as I was as wet as I could possibly get anyway. I reached the corner and immediately saw some taxis driving in the rain towards Haymarket Station down West Maitland Street.

The first two I tried to hail did not stop. They probably saw how wet I was and couldn't be bothered with a soaking interior. The third I tried to hail, however, did stop, and as I opened the door, the driver's hand reached back through the glass hatch with a copy of last night's *Evening News*.

"Can ye sit on this please, pal, yer drenched." I obliged, and unfolded the paper, sitting down on it.

I gave the driver Jackie's address. I really wanted to see her. I also wanted to go home and get some clothes from my own house, but I didn't have the courage to face my mother. I had left my hold-all at Ailsa's and I was not sure if this was a good idea. The bandage on my arm was soaking and the scar throbbed and stung.

I tipped the driver and apologized for being so damp, then walked along Jackie's street past the Dominion Theatre and to Jackie's front gate. The front garden was bisected by a long path to the front door of an impressively sized house, flanked by a gorgeously overgrown garden, made more beautiful by the asymmetry of its bushes and flowers. Her mother, I had been told, had doted on it, and Jackie had done her best to maintain it. Now, although it was by no means dying, or choked with weeds, she did not have the patience or know-how her mother had to shower mathematical and geographical accuracy upon the landscaping. Therefore, florid bushes hung over, weighted by their own deciduousness, creating small green perfumed tunnels for the local fauna to play and hunt within. A rock garden had become a shock of colours, speckled with occasional grey and little form. The front of the house was alive with ivy, seldom trimmed from its windows.

I walked around to the back. I had managed to rouse her this way before, one drunken night after a session at the Canny Man's. I scooped up some gravel from a small pile outside the kitchen door. It had to be just after six, maybe even later. She was probably awake. A solitary rook called and I scanned the back garden. The end was heavily wooded to provide a protective barrier against either winds or curious neighbours. The slightly overgrown grass gave the garden a lumpy appearance, like small green waves in a lake, mocking the positively Victorian-looking rusted lawn-roller parked and chronically unused at the wooded end.

The two sides of the back garden were thick bands of earth housing bushes, shrubs, and rushes; apart from that, four tall iron poles joined by ropes at the top stood in a square on the lawn about fifteen feet apart for hanging clothes to dry.

Jackie's was the top window on the right and I cast up my handful of gravel. It made a satisfying but soft crackle on the window, and sure enough, there she was. She waved down, expressionless, and disappeared from the window. A moment later I heard the huge key turn in the kitchen door lock and it swung open.

"Adam, you're wet through, come in." She had on a t-shirt and grey running shorts. "Let's go upstairs and you can take a shower in my bathroom. I'll fetch you something to wear." As we walked up the stairs, I realized how stupid it was to be here. I didn't know why I had come, except I was scared and I knew she was kind. How would I explain all of this?

I peeled off my damp clothes in the bathroom that was adjoining her bedroom. I then carefully peeled the bandage from my arm. The scar was closed, but looked like an angry red lightning bolt on my arm.

I turned on the shower and enjoyed the comforting heat.

There was a knock at the door. "I'm going to take your wet things and hang them up to dry. Here's a pair of Dad's trousers and an old t-shirt of yours you left ages ago." She placed them on the toilet seat.

"Thanks, Jackie."

I finished showering and dried myself off. Her father's cotton trousers almost fit me, but were a little loose around the waist. I couldn't remember when I had left the t-shirt.

I walked into her bedroom. She was sitting cross-legged on the bed reading. "So what happened?" she asked, looking up at me.

"I met someone, a girl, who I think is mental. I was at her house last night and she told me I couldn't see you or speak to you again. She was asking me about old girlfriends and, I mean, I just told her that we were still friends and it was good, and I was still fond of you, you know? As a friend. And then she fucking did this." I showed her my scarred forearm.

She gasped. "Oh my god, Adam. Who is she? Who would do this? Where did you meet her?"

"At the Royal Circus, the other night." I didn't want to let Jackie know I had been out scoring opium in some seedy flat near Leith Walk. I suddenly felt ashamed that I had let someone do this to me.

"Don't see her again. She's not well, no one does this sort of thing. I'm really glad you're fond of me, as I am you, but, I'm off to Aberdeen, really soon, and it's not like we see each other that much. You know, I knew you were off to see a girl the other day and I felt sad, and I missed you, hence the big sloppy kiss. I've felt really stupid ever since."

I laughed slightly. "Yeah, I wondered about that. I felt a bit weird, but it was nice, it was a nice thing," I sighed. "I left my bag there, I have to go back and get it."

"Well, then do so, just don't stay for dinner. Where does she live?"

"West End. Thank you, Jackie, you're a good friend."

"Happy to be, Adam. I'm glad you came when you did in the downpour. I couldn't really sleep and I was waiting for it to subside so I could go for a run. I'm glad I didn't miss you, you look exhausted, by the way. I'd say stay and take a nap, but if Dad notices, he'll be cross with me."

"Oh, I'm fine. I'm going to go and fetch my bag in a minute. Look, the sun's peeping out." And it was, the rain having been reduced to a slight drizzle.

"Are you working today?" she asked.

"I was fired yesterday, I let a friend walk out with some free booze," I sighed. I remembered the money in my pocket. "Where are my clothes? There's a bit of cash in the trouser pocket."

"They're hanging up in the kitchen. You can come back later this afternoon or tonight. Come for dinner, they'll be dry by then."

"Thanks, I will."

In the kitchen I pulled out a soaking ten, five, and one pound note and keys from the back pocket of my trousers that were hanging from a clotheshorse along with my shirt and socks.

"I'll see you later, yeah?" I said, and kissed Jackie on the cheek. I really didn't want to leave.

"You'll be all right Adam, just come back for dinner later, okay?"

"Thank you." Dinner, yes, but where would I go afterwards?

9 · CARAVAN MAN

The rain beats softly and then violently against the side and the roof of the caravan, as if it is ranting away to itself, and then all of a sudden, it makes a point, and becomes more vehement in its ranting. The wind howls its agreement.

Outside is a dark field as the afternoon comes to its conclusion. The heavy lead blanket of clouds has not shifted today.

The man sits at the kitchen table, the tiny kitchen table. You might be able to call it that. Really, what it is, is a Formica-topped square slab that folded down from the wall on two chains, like a drawbridge. The man is sobbing in and out gently. He has a shirt on, a tartan shirt. Red. He has no trousers on, just briefs. In and out goes the air from his mouth. Like a miniature version of the wind outside, he is mirroring the wind and the rain with his breathing and his tears.

"Uh wuh huh huh heeh."

"Uh wuh huh huh-h-h-h-h."

The last few sounds like he is almost trying to clear his throat, but there is nothing to clear, just sobs.

On the "table" is a hunting rifle, cartridges, a bottle of Bell's Scotch Whiskey (almost finished), a packet of twenty Embassy Number Ones (almost finished), a packet of Embassy Number Ones (unopened), and a cigarette lighter.

Between the sobs, howling and battering. Between the howling and battering, sobs.

"Ih ih ih ih, stolen fucking li-i-i-ife uh uh uh uh."

The man's face almost turns inside out with sobbing, lips curled up and down, nostrils flared. So much so he throws up a little on the table. Amber with pale yellow lumps. It just sort of squirts out, leaving a rope of vomit hanging from the right bottom lip as he cries more and little rivers of green snot start to pour slowly from his nostrils.

"Every fuckin' time. EVERY fuckin' ti-i-i-i-ime. Noooooooooo!"

Both hands collapse on the gun. It looks like he is tired and he is just grabbing the rifle for a pillow, because his head bows towards it.

"Ey, ey, ey hy hy hyyyyyy."

White caravan in darkness, the rain and the wind have won over everything. The howling and beating. Caravan seen from the other side of the field. A quick flash of light seen from behind one of the windows. No sound. Sound drowned out by the weather's untamed emotions.

10 · FORBIDDEN COLOURS

"Why did you leave? I was so worried when I woke up. Where have you been, darling? God, it's so wet outside!" Her voice had a soft, cooing scold to it as she stood at the door, pulling my heart out again, her vibrant red hair dishevelled, her half-asleep eyes, smiling and bringing a sweet texture to her face. Her arms draped themselves around my neck and she kissed me as she pulled me into the flat.

Turning to her bed, she let me go and disrobed. Her hair hung down in thin stalactites across the top of her back, a moving sculpture of muscle and utter tranquillity.

"Come back to bed, angel, will you?" and I undressed and slid under the covers. My hands found her waist and I still couldn't believe the way she felt, almost like a warm, sweet ghost, too perfect to be flesh. The last few hours fell away and I loved her so much that I would do whatever I had to in order to keep her. I no longer could piece together in my mind why I had left and why I had felt the way I did earlier. The feeling must have belonged to someone else, some interloper creeping into my psyche and polluting, pissing all over a fragile but colossal adoration. But here I was at home, breathing her in and out until I fell into a heavy slumber.

She was sitting up in bed when I awoke. "Where did you go this morning?" she asked without looking at me. There was nothing accusatory in her voice.

"I went home. I wanted to get a couple of things."

"Like what?"

"Well, nothing, as it happens. My mother locked the door from the inside and it meant I would have to ring the bell to get in and wake her and she would have just started screaming at me. It's a trick she used to use on my dad and I recently graduated to that status, I suppose."

"Does she shout at you a lot?"

"Oh, she's fucking barking mad."

"Adam, name it, I can get it for you, just ask."

"I had wanted to get some clothes, really."

"Well let's go to Princes Street and I'll buy you some clothes. I want to have a look as well. Would you like to?"

"I'd love to."

"It's half past eleven, let's go now."

We got up and I pulled on Jackie's father's trousers and my old t-shirt. A chill went through me when I realised that they were not the clothes I had left here in, hours ago, then I relaxed. Ailsa couldn't know that unless she had gone through my zipped-up hold-all, which remained where I had left it. She had clearly been asleep the whole time I was away, and for all she knew, I'd stuffed yesterday's clothes in there. I would have to get them back from Jackie later; I would not be able to explain losing them if it ever came up. This meant I would have to leave again. Plus, I had told Jackie I would come for dinner.

The rain had stopped and the city smelled fresh. High mother-of-pearl clouds stretched across the sky, and the even temperature made the early afternoon somewhat weatherless. We walked up Shandwick Place, hand in hand. The novelty was thrilling, as I felt her hand fondling mine. Princes Street was busy, the usual tourist hustle and bustle of Edinburgh in the summer before the Festival, when things went really mad.

Ailsa tugged my arm. "This one!" she smiled, pulling me into a department store. "Do you mind looking at girls' clothes with me here?"

"No, of course not. Let's go!"

A heavy aroma of mixed perfumes and makeup assaulted the senses upon entry. It was a smell I had known my whole life from touring these shops with my mother, as familiar as the early morning smell of malt and hops from the Scottish & Newcastle Brewery I would relish on my way to school every day.

We took the lift up to the women's department. It was quietly busy, not like a Saturday afternoon or Christmas. I followed Ailsa around. What else could I possibly do? There was little of interest for me here, but I was happy to look at the things Ailsa would pick off the racks. A few dresses of varying styles, a couple of blouses, a few other things.

"Okay, I can only take in three items at a time, so here, you take these," she said, separating a couple of blouses and handing them to me. "I'll try these on, then you can come in a couple of minutes later and tell me you've picked out some more things. They won't care, they won't notice, and we can pretend we're married." She said the last phrase with a mischievous grin, leaned towards me, and kissed me on the lips. She turned around and marched off to the dressing rooms. I looked at her with complete adoration. Every movement, although effortless, looked like it had been written for her by the greatest writer, or painted for her by the greatest painter. She was God and she was driving me and all the other women in the department insane, I could feel it.

I wandered about for a couple of minutes, feeling mildly awkward, and then walked towards the changing rooms. The attendant was patiently trying to explain to a non-English-speaking customer that she could only try on three garments at a time, with little success. I simply walked past her. She either didn't notice me or understandably assumed that I was a husband or boyfriend.

"Ailsa!" I whispered.

"Over here!" A clicking as the door unlatched, I slipped in. She was wearing the same clothes she had gone in with.

"Lock the door, angel," she said.

She looked at me with what I took as a kind of childish expectation. "Will you do something for me, Adam?"

"Sure, what?" I said, laughing.

"Try this on for me." She handed me a shiny silver-grey evening dress.

"What, you mean I put it on?"

"Yes."

"Ailsa, I'll rip it in two, I..."

"No you won't, and if you do, I'll buy it. I chose it specially for you, it'll almost fit, darling, I promise. Don't be a spoilsport and I'll make it really, really, really worth your while." She looked at me, smiling, wide-eyed and with her tongue overlapping her top front teeth.

I took off my shoes and trousers.

"She didn't even notice you, did she? Little missy out there."

"Nope. Can I leave on my shirt?"

"Fuck, no. Get it off."

I was naked and it was a strange, but not alien feeling. It was a bit like the swimming baths, one tiny door separating you from the rest of the public. However, this was a lot more exciting.

She had unzipped the dress and held it for me as I stepped in and pushed my arms through the short sleeves. Behind me, Ailsa leaned into my ear and whispered, "Hold in your tummy." Her breath, slight and warm, aroused me immediately and I felt myself pressed up against the slick material. She slowly zipped me up. It was tight, and I knew if I bent down, it would split; if I walked, it would probably burst at the seams. From behind again, I felt her tie a scarf around my eyes, one of the items she had picked to try on. "Stay very, very still," and I heard her move around in front of me. Was she kneeling? I felt her hand reach up inside the dress and cup my balls, my erection felt like it was going to rip a hole in the front of the dress. Her soft hand stroked it almost imperceptibly at first, getting a tiny bit stronger every time.

"These trousers and that shirt weren't in your bag last night, and if you didn't get them from your house, I wonder where you got them from at five in the morning. Hmm, angel?"

The molten sweetness of her hand on me drowned out the universe. I didn't hear her, there were just 'word shapes' in the air, sensual textures falling from her sweet mouth. Then it hit me, like a wave of electricity shaking my whole body. My erection shrivelled and I pulled the scarf from my eyes, blurry, not her face? Her face? It was completely changed, her hair on the face of a demon. Tight, white lips, bulging eyes.

"Do you think I am fucking stupid?" A pause of solid concrete, no breathing, no air. "You were with her, I know you were, I can smell it, or did you shower in the rain? That perfume! That CUNT!"

Horrific image of myself in the dressing room mirror, grotesquely squeezed into a tiny evening dress, twisted red face, ugly and frightened, my mouth jawing the words that I could not say, like a fish on a slab of stone before beheading.

Ailsa bent down and picked up my clothes, unlocked the dressing room door, and walked out.

"Ailsa!" I said in a loud whisper. "I had to go there, I was soaking, she lives near me, I needed to borrow something to wear, these are her dad's trousers, he was there, even! Honest to Christ, they let me take a shower, who wouldn't?" There was silence. Was she there? I daren't open the door, my look was not a sympathetic one.

"Ailsa! Ailsa! Ailsa!" I harshly whispered into nothing. There was nothing to do, there was nothing to wear: the other clothes she had chosen were hanging up, tiny dresses and blouses. I stood, unthinking—what was there to think? Nothing.

"Sir, please come out of the changing room now, or we will be forced to unlock the door from the outside. We will call the police, sir."

My jaw dropped. Such an amazingly perfect setup, so perfect the execution. Because I was an idiot and I was a liar.

My breathing, hot and fast as I fumbled with the latch on the door. "Do– do– don't call the police! Fuckin' hell, I can explain. Fuck, me and my girlfriend had a fight, she made me come in here. Oh Christ."

I opened the door to the impassive faces of the attendant and the store detective. The attendant, the one who had barely noticed me, and probably Ailsa as well, couldn't have been more than 20, with her hair in the sort of fake rockabilly style that was popular at the time. She had a bland, annoying, wide-eyed expression that made her look moronic. The store detective was about my mother's age, short with a two-piece navy blue business suit on, black hair in a bob, a hooked nose. Exactly how they could look at me so expressionlessly whilst I was the picture of ridicule and humiliation, I don't know. Perhaps they saw this kind of thing every day.

"Come with us, please, sir," said the detective, and what choice did I have? I had no clothes and nowhere to run. Tears were streaming down my face. The detective seemed to take a little pity on me. "The office is just around the corner sir, no one will notice, just keep your head down."

I followed them out of the dressing room area, and as we walked out onto the shop floor, I saw my clothes crumpled against the attendant's desk. "That's them! Those are my clothes, there!" The attendant pulled a plastic shopping bag from behind her desk and stuffed the clothes into it.

The office was a matter of feet away from the attendant's desk. Once inside the cramped room, I was asked to sit down at a desk and told to wait whilst the detective and the attendant left. "We're going to be right outside the door, so please do not try and leave or we'll call the police. You may put your clothing back on." This was delivered by the detective in a slightly world-weary tone. Perhaps this was not such an unusual occurrence and, for some reason, this gave me a little hope.

They left and I heard them talking outside, the older woman's voice considerably deeper than the younger. I couldn't decipher anything they were talking about. I wondered where Ailsa was, and what the consequences of my actions would be for us.

I removed the dress as carefully as I could. There was no damage that I could see, but my heart sank as I noticed a tiny stain where the end of my penis had been: the material had stretched there, leaving a three- or four-inch oval bulge. Of course they would notice it and, of course, I didn't have any way of paying for it.

A few minutes later, they came back in. I had sat back down at the desk and the detective sat down opposite me whilst the attendant stood at her back.

"What is your full name, sir?" she asked, pulling a piece of paper that looked like a questionnaire from a ring binder.

"Adam Joseph Kelvin," I answered, my name sounding ridiculous against the actions of the last ten minutes.

She wrote it down on the top of the page. "Mr. Kelvin, Miss Patterson here claims that she did not see either you or your companion enter the changing rooms." She raised her eyes from the page and looked at me.

"I snuck in after Ailsa, that's my girlfriend. She told me to, she wanted to try on more clothes than she was allowed, so she told me to bring them in. I just walked in, Miss Patterson was trying to explain something to a foreign woman." I didn't want to get Miss Patterson into trouble, but I needed some kind of an ally, however tenuous.

The detective wrote something down. "Can you describe your companion for us, Mr. Kelvin?"

"Yes, she's about five foot two or three, long red hair, about to the middle of her shoulder blades, very slim, very good-looking, she was wearing a black leather motorbike jacket and blue jeans, with a white t-shirt. She's eighteen."

"What is your address?"

"22 Jordan Lane. It's in Morningside."

"Mr. Kelvin, Miss Patterson has no recollection of someone entering the dressing room at that time just before you. Granted, though, she was trying to assist a non-English-speaking customer." She turned to Miss Patterson. "Do you remember a person that fits the description Mr. Kelvin just submitted?"

"No, I didn't see anyone leave fitting that description."

"Well," I looked from one to the other, "I didn't just decide to come in and try on a dress, she sneaked out, didn't she? This whole thing is a setup, I admit I did something really, really stupid, but she gave us all the slip. She's probably on her way back home laughing her head off. How else would my clothes get out there? Are you saying I took them off before I let myself in?" The same expressionless faces offered no answers or, mercifully perhaps, opinions.

·I realised how completely insane I sounded, and yes, perhaps I did take off all my clothes, perhaps, in their eyes, I was a complete pervert! I put my head in my hands on the desk. "I know how this sounds, I'm an idiot, but I'm not some fucking pervert, honestly. I'm really sorry, I'll do anything, just, please..." My voice trailed off as I realized that she was writing and probably not listening to a word I was saying.

"Are you currently employed, Mr. Kelvin?" she asked.

"I was, up until yesterday, at Safeway's in Morningside."

"Why are you no longer employed there?"

"I'm going to University in September, and I wanted a little free time before I leave." I was hoping that they wouldn't call, I was really chancing it here.

"Mr. Kelvin, have you ever been charged with an offence before?"

"No."

"Public indecency?"

I was panicked. "Oh, Christ, no, not at all! I just left school. No one was hurt... I was messing around!"

"Yes, no one was hurt, Mr. Kelvin, but there were complaints of a male voice and a male presence in the women's changing rooms. Now, the way I see it, you snuck in there to try on women's clothing, for a thrill, or maybe to draw attention to yourself, which you certainly managed to do."

"She was here! She lives in Palmerston Place, her name is Ailsa McCann, she's probably in Princes Street Gardens right now."

She stopped writing and sighed, pausing for a few seconds while she tapped a fingertip on the desktop.

"Okay, do I have your word that you will never set foot in this establishment again?"

She looked me in the eye.

"Absolutely," I replied.

"All right," she said, capping the pen and putting the paper back into the ring binder. She looked up at me and pointed. "I don't want anything more to do with you, or with this sordid situation. Leave, please, as quickly as possible."

"Yes, thank you."

"Everyone on staff will be briefed with a full description. If you are ever seen on the premises again, the police will be alerted immediately. Is that clear?"

"Of course. I'm truly sorry, you'll never see me again."

I got up, my body awash in warm rivers of relief. I couldn't believe my good luck, and that they had not inspected the dress. I would be lost before they could look at it properly. Perhaps they would send a bill—they had my address—but for now, I was free.

I left the shop and was immediately in the fast, bustling foot traffic of Princes Street... anonymous again. I had some thinking to do, but realized quickly that I had little choice here but to throw myself at her mercy. I had nothing but the clothes that I was wearing, my wallet was back at her flat. How long would she stay angry for? Every few seconds I would see that horrible image of myself in the dressing room mirror: the red mottled face, the body too big for the dress, the straining and stretching of the crotch, Ailsa spitting "that cunt" with such venom, like a stinging snake bite. What had she done? I couldn't believe it; it was different from the knife incident, not an act of compulsive rage, but one of creeping suspicion and cold revenge, propelled by a whiplash temper.

I had lied.

I should not have lied.

Lying had always been the easy way out.

Now it was not.

Ailsa knew.

I had to forget about Jackie. Ailsa would not accept Jackie on any level.

I was covered in Ailsa, my entire skin was covered in her and the pull was far too strong, I should have realised how much I needed her and how greedy I was for her.

She has a short temper.

Well, don't do anything to ignite it.

You can manage that can't you, you idiot?

I cursed myself again, this time for not having any cigarettes. I had veered off the main road to Rose Street, a narrow street that ran parallel to Princes Street. It was busy with lunch-goers and early drinkers visiting the various pubs. I really wanted a drink. I walked around Charlotte Square and down Queensferry Street to Chester Street, the street of the argument I had witnessed Ailsa's parents engaged in, and then to Palmerston Place. I walked up to her door at the back and knocked. If she was home, what if she didn't answer? Why should she, apart from the fact that I had learned my lesson. I felt I had endured punishment enough, but perhaps I was being too lenient on myself, Ailsa may well have thought very differently.

I waited. Utter silence. Should I go to the front door and try and persuade her parents to let me grab my wallet? They had never seen me, I could be anyone. If she had really wanted to punish me, she could have discarded my clothes in one of the many litter bins up and down Princes Street, leaving me with nothing, I could have been in jail right now, wearing a dress.

I knocked on the door again, nothing, again, nothing. There was no letter box, so I just spoke to the door. "Ailsa, I just need my wallet. I'm sorry. Just let me get my stuff and I'll leave you alone."

A huge almighty void of silence. It even sounded like all traffic had stopped in deference to Ailsa's wishes, or to my shame. She wasn't home. She was out shopping, mocking me in her mind, the ridiculous lying Adam, in his too-small dress. Maybe she'd come home in a few hours, laden with shopping bags. She'd see me and sigh, forgive me, let me in to drink wine and look at her new clothes. I would never talk about or see Jackie again.

I continued to wait. Silence. Nothing stirred in the garden. I walked out onto Palmerston Place, still not a soul. I walked to West Maitland Street and back. I didn't want to wait in the garden. What if she saw me and decided to call the police in another act of rage? Even more realistically, what if one of her parents saw me?

So I walked around the block, again and again: West Maitland Street, Grovesnor Street, Lansdowne Crescent, over and over. This was hell, the repetition, like Prometheus, the horrific blend of panic, pain and extreme boredom. It almost occurred to me to just walk to Jackie's—at least I was guaranteed a meal, and to hell with the consequences.

I saw a phone box. What was the number she had written down? It was in my wallet of course. I had no coins, but I would hear her pick up before the pips went. Oh! Just to hear "hello?" in her voice before PIP-PIP-PIP-PIP! 556 0923? I was certain the last four numbers started with a zero.

I opened the door of the phone box, picked up the receiver and dialled 556 0923.

Brrrrrp. Brrrrp-Brrrrp. Brrrrp-Brrrrp. Brrrrp. (click) "Hello?" A young man's deep voice, lazily mocking, too young to be a father's voice. If this was the correct number, then this had to be a boyfriend, someone she'd called up to replace me. I slammed the receiver down and picked it up again, dialling the number one more time. It rang longer this time. (click) "Hello?" Same deep voice, same inflection— was that a bit of a laugh, though? The way it fell out of his mouth, the first syllable rushing out, as if riding on the crest of a hearty guffaw? There's no way she called someone and had them come to her so quickly. In my mind I quickly saw two different scenarios that were happening in her flat right now. The first had this guy sitting on the side of her bed, naked, save for a sheet covering his privates, holding the telephone and smiling, Ailsa lying languidly, stretched out on the bed, head resting on her arm, smiling and giggling. The second and far preferable image was of Ailsa sitting on her living room floor in semi-darkness and complete silence, waiting. I had to have the wrong number!

One more time, just to make sure, just one more time. I picked up the receiver gingerly, as if they would be able to tell and could get in position for a good laugh.

I gently dialled the number, my fingers almost careless as they tried to appear nonchalant.

556 0923. Brrrrp-Brrrrp. Brrrrp-Brrrrp. It went on and on this time. Were they making love? No answer. On and on, perfectly symmetrical pairs of rings on a black static motorway into a void. Brrrrp-Brrrrp. Brrrrp-Brrrrp. They were fucking their brains out. I smashed the receiver into the cradle, over and over again, a high-pitched keening shriek coming from my mouth as I did so. I stopped myself. I had not broken it, the sturdy black plastic was too tough for me to crack. I looked at it as the recent violence swirled around the confined space. Hard breathing. I bet I had the wrong number. When Ailsa was ready to see me again, I would discreetly check her phone number and satisfy myself, just take a look at that paper in my wallet. Everything would be fine.

It was now mid-to-late afternoon by my reckoning. I was starving. It started to rain again, the rain bringing with it a chill, one that I was unprepared for. I needed to walk away from here. Ailsa had the means to basically do as she pleased; she might be on a train on her way anywhere right now, she could be with another man, who knew? I didn't want to become suspicious to the local residents—I did not in any way look "moneyed"—so I walked to the Dean Village and to the water of Leith and the same spot we had picnicked in a few days before.

Should I go home and knock on the door? Face my mother? It seemed almost reasonable, but something in me wanted to gamble on seeing Ailsa, seeing her come and look for me later perhaps, or for me to run into her and for her heart to fill with pity and fondness for me. I wanted to be outside here, really. If I was not in her arms, in her place, then I would sit and say nothing and I would eat nothing and I would be happy to waste away without her. I was resolute.

I sat down by the river in the rain. A tree offered a little shelter, but I was enjoying the cold drops as they fell on me. I enjoyed the forward motion of the river as it was pelted with the tiny raindrops. The sound had a soothing meditative quality to it and, very soon, time disappeared from the whole equation, it seemed to be the same few seconds, over and over. The light was dull rather than soft, but it was lulling along with the crystalline percussion of rain on water, the sound of unending business and purpose. It eventually made me lie down and close my eyes.

When I awoke, it was still light. The rain had stopped, the sound of a lone crow had roused me, but very quickly I realised that things were very wrong. I was parched, my throat felt like dry wood with glass shards embedded in its walls. My joints ached—actually, my whole body ached. I was shivering violently and my skin felt like it had been burned or stung by thousands of wasps. My head was hard to move, such was the headache I was suffering, a molten unmoored rock rolling around in my skull. Ailsa's voice, exaggerated in a loop going round and round, crossed with Jackie's voice: "That perfume, that cunt, that perfume, that cunt," "I'll fetch you something to wear, I'll fetch you something to wear," resolving in both their voices escalating in pitch to absurd proportions and gibberish and then back again.

At first I didn't realize that I was outside. I had no idea what the time of day was, it may have been dusk. I was too disorientated. I thought I was in the Morningside Cemetery and I could walk to Jackie's, but then realized that there was no river in the cemetery. When I got my bearings and knew where I was, I tried to get up. Shooting pain through my back and a strong feeling of nausea made me lie down again. I was very ill, I had to get to Ailsa's, she would at least show me the mercy of helping me back home or something. If she wasn't home, I'd have to throw myself at the mercy of her parents.

I walked slowly back to Palmerston Place, pausing only to steady myself against a wall while I threw up clear liquid (there was no food to throw up, and very little liquid). The subsequent retching made me feel like I was cramping every muscle in my body. Every step I took sent violent painful shudders through me, so I walked very slowly and as lightly as I could. A few people looked quite horrified as they passed me; I must have looked like I was drunk.

When I eventually reached her house, I noticed that the blackout shutters were still in place from this morning. This was probably a bad sign. I knocked on her door feebly.

"Ailsa, please," I said as loudly as I could. Nothing. I had to sit down, but sitting down was too painful on my spine, so I just curled up outside her door. I was freezing cold and my head was throbbing quickly in tandem with my heart. The pain in my throat was such that I could not swallow. I tried to reach out and knock on the door, but I could barely scrape my knuckles.

I must have passed out again, because I was awoken by Ailsa. It was very dark, and the light that shone from her flat through the open door hurt my eyes badly. I couldn't focus but she was kneeling beside me stroking my brow. "Adam, wake up, please wake up." She sounded a bit scared.

"I'm sorry, Ailsa." My voice didn't sound like my voice, it was harsh and alien to my ears, foreign, the way my mouth moved was strange, and talking made my head hurt with stabbing pains.

"Try to get up and walk to the bed, Adam, you have a really high fever. You can take a bath and get out of these clothes, they're soaking wet."

Slowly I got to my feet, Ailsa helping me. We walked very slowly into her flat.

"Let's just go into the bathroom and I'll wash you."

We slowly walked into the bathroom and I sat down on the toilet whilst she turned the water on. She then helped me out of my shirt, as I stood up shakily to get my trousers off. Putting much of my weight on her shoulders with an arm, I got into the bath. The water was cool, not cold. "I'm going to try and get your fever down, angel."

I shivered and she started to sponge me down, rubbing the sponge with soap and gently rubbing me with the sponge.

"I'm going to wash your hair," she said, and filled a pint glass with water, pouring it over my head.

"I panicked when you cut me. I'm so stupid, Ailsa."

"Don't talk, angel, I'm going to make it better." She massaged shampoo into my hair and then rinsed it clean.

"Here, take these aspirin, okay?" She popped two white pills into my mouth and gave me a tooth mug of water to wash them down. The pain from swallowing was excruciating. I held the side of the bath and stood up whilst Ailsa wrapped a towel around me and gently patted me dry.

"I'll put you to bed and I'll be right there for you when you wake up."

"What time is it?"

"It's about ten, angel. I was here all day. I'm sorry, I thought you'd just eventually run back to her. I was so angry, but then about half an hour ago I heard you cry out in your sleep and I realized you were right outside. It took me ages to wake you up. I'm so sorry. God, you're so ill, Adam."

"I just want to go to bed."

"Of course, come on, let's go."

She led me to the bed and I fell asleep almost immediately. My dreams drowned in the deep darkness of the water of Leith. I was falling down the side of the valley, the shingle and shale giving me nothing to hold on to. I was naked when I fell into the water, black and punctuated with glowing tiny red eyes, strange eels and fish violently knocking into me, the material of the dress from earlier pulled over my head, my hands flailing.

I woke up soaking wet and screaming.

"Adam, Adam. You're okay, you're all right now, it was a dream."

Ailsa was beside me on the bed, cross-legged. Waves of relief swept through me.

"You're an angel."

"I'm Ailsa." She smiled and touched the side of my face. "We need to change these sheets and you need to have another bath. I think you've sweated through everything. Come on."

I got out of bed slowly and she once again helped me into the bathroom. Sitting me down on the toilet, she drew another bath.

"What time is it now?"

"It's three or four I think. Do you feel any better?"

"A little bit."

"You'll be okay in a few hours, I bet."

"I think my fever has broken."

I managed to get into the bath myself.

"I'm going upstairs to find some more sheets, I'll be right back."

I sat in the bath and made half-hearted attempts to wash myself. My mind, still a little feverish, threw up images of the riverbank where I had lain down, the store detective, the ruined dress.

I heard Ailsa return and recognized the soft crack of sheets being unfolded with a single movement of the arms. I got out of the bath and braced myself against the bathroom door as I began to feel a little faint. I breathed, focused, and walked out of the bathroom. I lay down on the bed as she was picking up the old sheets.

"Go back to sleep, angel," she said, and I did.

The dreams were not as violent this time. They were disturbing and still, but they didn't make me wake.

The next time I woke up, the shutters were open and light saturated the room, bring out the most intense colours from everything Ailsa owned.

Ailsa was at her desk, drawing, wearing a short robe. "Hello," she smiled. "I drew you, d'you want to see it?" She brought it over: it was me lying in bed with my hands behind my head. It was good.

"It's amazing! I look quite well!"

"Oh, you looked so peaceful, like you didn't give a toss about anything!" she smiled. "Are you feeling all right, then?"

"Like I've been kicked by a horse, but I'm a lot better."

"Do you want to eat something?" she asked.

"No, not yet. I'd love a cup of tea, though."

"I'll go and stick the kettle on," and she left to go upstairs.

I was far too weak to question all of this. Did she want to forget the whole business of the setup in the women's changing rooms? Would we both let it be forgotten for the sake of this—well, this idyll? She had moved from the most focused, steely rage into a selfless, yielding nurse.

She came back downstairs with a tray, two mugs, a teapot and a small milk jug. She set it down on the floor near the bed, then lifted the stylus onto the record that was on the turntable of her record player. Immediately there was a lightly busy, but not ferocious dialogue between a cello and a piano.

"What's this?" I asked.

"Beethoven, Cello Sonata Number 3."

"It's beautiful. Do you play anything?"

"Piano, for years."

"I'd love to hear that one day."

"One day."

"Are things all right between us, Ailsa?"

"I don't want to talk about that just now, angel. Everything's fine, okay?"

"Okay," I said, but with the faintest hint of a question in my voice.

I sat up in bed and enjoyed the sun and the room awash with the cello and the piano as she poured out our tea.

"You don't take sugar do you?" she asked.

"Oh no," I said absently.

"You should spend the day in bed, then maybe tomorrow we can do something, maybe you'll be all better." There was a touch of child in her hopeful tone.

"Oh, I'll be fine tomorrow, I'll be just fine."

"We could go on a picnic or something."

"I'd love to."

"We could go up the Pentlands if it doesn't rain, or the beach. We'll see."

The events of the rest of the day were few and were ushered in and out of my consciousness with a soft serenity. She drew and I slept. Later on, she turned on the radio quietly and, as the light outside began to dim, she came and lay down beside me, stroking my forehead.

"You should have something to eat," she said.

"Oh, oh, god, well, maybe I could manage a bit of toast," I replied apprehensively.

"I'll go and make some in a minute, I just want to lie with you here just now."

She lay down beside me and said nothing for a few minutes.

"I'm sorry I played that cruel trick on you, Adam, and it's all my fault you're so ill, and we'll talk no more of it, okay?" Her voice sank to a whisper. "I think you should stay with me here, and fuck the outside world, fuck everybody, you see what happens when anyone else is involved even in the smallest way? It rocks the boat, baby. And your old life, I don't think you care very much about your old life, do you, Adam?"

Right then, I didn't, as she whispered softly into my ear. I could feel the warmth of her breath, its damp sweetness heralding her almost words into me. Right then, I didn't, the warmth of her body beside my sickness was melting away my past quickly. She had destroyed me absolutely and then saved me with such striking mercy. She was God, she was God, she was God.

"I don't want to talk about my past, or feel it ever again. I've almost completely forgotten it, it isn't there." I let my hand drowsily wander under her shirt. "What about your parents? What will they think of this guy in the basement?"

"You'll hardly ever see them. I want our world, Adam, this is our wee island, our sky is on the roof, our wine and our roses."

After a few minutes she got up and disappeared upstairs. I felt a lot better; swallowing was a dull ache rather than a barbed minefield of shattering glass, and I realized when I sat up that I was actually quite hungry after all. She returned ten minutes later with the tray, the teapot, mugs, and a plate with four pieces of toast on it; there was also a butter dish and butter knife. Placing the tray on the ground, she smoothed the bedclothes and then placed the tray beside me on the bed. Nothing was uttered as she poured tea and I ate a dry piece of toast, wary of the butter, not wishing to push my luck.

"What do you feel like? Do you want to do anything?" she asked. "I'll read to you if you want."

"That'd be nice. What did you have in mind?"

"Ever read *The Story of the Eye*?"

I had, it had turned me on and repulsed me. Its extremism had excited me so much, but what was more exciting was to think that Ailsa had read it, that it had turned her on like it had me. I had to hear her read it.

"I loved it. Read it to me in your voice, Ailsa."

She picked the book up from her desk and brought it over. Sitting cross-legged on the bed, she started reading from a seemingly random point. Her enunciation and intonation matched her physique, the words were the most complex ballet moves, articulated and accomplished with an innocent determination, lulling and busy, playful, her voice skipped and slid smoothly over my skin, like the ghost of a silk scarf at lightning speed. Her tongue lightly wrapped itself around incredible perversions, incredible anatomies, and incredibly beautiful people. Any trace of illness was eroded by an overpowering feeling to have her. Now.

It was not long before we were making love. She climbed on top of me with skill and a reverent gentleness, aware of my weakened and fragile state, moving slowly—in fact, barely moving at all. Her infinity eyes fixed on mine, the most beautiful face I'd ever seen, the most vulnerable and dominating at the same time, her dark fringe of hair moved gently over her eyes, one hand on my chest as I cupped the side of her face.

"Promise me, Adam," she said with barely audible urgency, coming to a dead stop.

"Promise you what, darling?"

She squeezed her legs together very slightly, yet giving me a tidal wave of yearning pleasure. Then she stopped again, bending her face down to mine. She kissed me, lips sweet and wet, she whispered in my ear. "Promise me everything, Adam. Promise me you'll do what I want and this'll be yours all the time, you can do what you want to me, anything."

An incredibly slight squeeze that she maintained without the slightest perceptible movement. All of a sudden, I was levitating slowly, floating as she resumed movement on top of me, rotating in minute increments. The sweet ache was unbearable.

"Do you promise, Adam?" Dead stop.

"Yes, anything, anything, anything."

She took one of my hands and put it on her breast, placing her hand over my eyes, she squeezed her legs sharply together and bent down quickly to cover my mouth with hers.

I was looking down on us from above the bed as I came hard inside her. I inhaled sharply, then my breath came out in loud sharp bursts.

"Sleep now, baby," she said as she climbed off, and I think I was asleep before she had done so.

11 • ENDLESS SOUL

The next few days saw the creation of our world. The day after my promise, I woke up next to Ailsa feeling sanctified, whole, holy, enlightened. It was as if someone, in one simple movement, had handed me the instructions to my life, and they were not complicated.

I woke up next to Ailsa and felt relief and genuine pity for those who did not, but at the same time knowing that I would never have the need to speak to these people, or for that matter, anyone really. Our world.

We made love in the steamy darkness of her shuttered room beneath the covers, then rose like civilized animals to eat, slurping back cold orange juice from a carton and gnawing a baguette, both of which she'd fetched from the kitchen upstairs. No words were exchanged, they need not have been, each understood perfectly their role. We made love again after breakfast. Any concept from the outside became first absurd, then abstract, and then gone over the hours that followed. As I became consumed with our eroticism, we swayed, drunk on ourselves as the shutters on the windows banned time. Occasionally, Ailsa would put on a record and we would laugh when we realized later on that the side had ended, and our lives were taking rhythmic form around the click/hiss of the needle stuck in the runout groove of the LP.

There was no interruption from upstairs, it was merely our source for sustenance, as Ailsa would spirit herself up there for wine, fruit and bread every so often. Soon the days disappeared, then the nights. At one point she went upstairs and returned a few minutes later with a bottle of wine, a bag of oranges, and a dozen white roses. "They were lying by the kitchen sink. I'll put them in water." She lay them down on the bed. "Someone told me once it was bad luck to have white roses in your bedroom," she said idly, "Utter rubbish, I hope." She shrugged off her robe and, picking up the roses again, she moved towards the bathroom, looking briefly over her shoulder at me. She looked incredible without any grooming, unkempt as a forest animal, and as hungry. The hunger in her eyes was mixed with a mocking tenderness. Her hair, dishevelled, was somehow at odds with her figure, which had the symmetry and splendour of crafted crystal. But her face, again her face, carried with it incredible wealth, and the predatory urge of a wild animal.

"Come back here." I stated quietly. It was not as a command, more like a decision we had made together without having to consult or ponder over. Without hesitation she came back, throwing the roses upwards in an exaggerated movement. It seemed we had coupled before they even hit the floor. It was quick this time, violent and strong, and afterwards we lay on the ground panting. She opened the wine and we passed it back and forth between each other, drinking deeply.

"Do you want to take some acid?" she asked.

"Erm... okay, okay let's, I'll need cigs though."

"We'll get some. Let's drop it and go on an adventure."

"Where? Outside?"

"Yeah, why not? We could take the blue glass head and some supplies."

"Not the Dean Village."

"No, of course not, angel, no Dean Village."

"What about the Pentlands? Hillend? Or maybe the Braidburn Valley?"

These were all haunts of mine that I had used with friends for smoking hash or tripping. Hillend, the gateway to the Pentland Hills at the south of the city was a fantastic locale for picking magic mushrooms in the early autumn weeks. It also boasted a ski run, which had provided amusement in the past.

She got up and went to the blackout shutters, throwing them open. The sunlight was glorious and came as a real shock to the system. "Oh, I forgot to mention, it's Sunday morning," she laughed. "When I went upstairs the last time I got a real fright, I thought it was the wee hours! Let's take this acid and go to church. It's amazing, it'll be hilarious."

"Can we smoke in church?" I joked.

"Oh, if you're with me you can do anything you like, angel, anything," she deadpanned back.

She opened a drawer in her dresser and pulled out a small, square wax paper envelope. She brought it over to me and opened it under my nose.

"Look, d'you see them? They're called Armadas, there's a little Spanish galleon on each one, see?"

There were four of them, making a square of about an inch, each acid tablet split by perforations from the other. As far as I knew, this was "blotter acid" and, in my experience, could either be really strong, or just as easily, weak. The last acid I had taken had a Japanese flag on it and had done nothing.

"Hang on," she said, and went upstairs, grabbing her robe as she went. She returned with a carton of orange juice. She carefully separated two of the acid tabs, put one on her tongue, and washed it down with a generous mouthful of orange juice. She handed me the acid, and the juice, and I did the same.

"We can go to Saint Mary's first, and then come back and get our supplies. It's just down the street."

Without washing, we threw on our clothes, a little drunk from the wine, and giggling together. We left the flat to the sound of the cathedral bells' joyous clang permeating the clean bright morning. We felt exultant, hand in hand. We could see a throng of churchgoers outside walking into the cathedral, or milling about talking. Mostly older people dressed up in the pastel colours I have always associated with church; the men, though, in sober greys and blacks.

We were about to do something that felt mischievous, but not bad, and I felt at peace with Ailsa, strong. Outside God's house, with the girl who had brought me back from such sickness and who had spoiled me by lavishing her body on me, trapping me in luxury I had only ever fantasized over.

We entered after most of the rest had done so. I felt the first remote electrical pulses of the drug we had taken and, as we walked in, I glanced up with some awe at the spire, which was dramatic and forbidding in its staggering height.

Inside, I drew my breath sharply. The stained glass windows seemed as high as the spire, towering behind the altar, which was in itself the size of a small house, seemingly. The sounds of the people sitting in the pews were dwarfed by the silence of the god that seemed to fill the room. The sounds of the people were those of toys, miniature models of people and rusty clockwork mice, unworthy of presence of this greatness. Ailsa squeezed my hand and I knew it was a sign, she was feeling the same gently throbbing voltage through her nerves as well. The acid was starting to take effect. It was like when I was young and bolted into the Big Dipper or the Octopus at Whitley Bay and I knew there was no going back, and what was coming would be overpowering and frightening.

Ailsa put her mouth to my ear. "God's watching you, Adam, you're a butterfly on a fucking pin."

I couldn't possibly tell if she was serious or not, such was the strength of the acid, but I was knocked by a tidal wave of fear which, once it had run over me, didn't seem to go away. The back of the altar housed pale sandy-coloured statues. It was impossible to tell whether they were male or female, if they were shaking in exultation and smiling, or if they were quivering in fear and pain. I did know that they were all looking at me, moist shining black eyes behind the stone faces. My god, there were children trapped back there!

"Ailsa, there's kids trapped in the altar, do you see?" I whispered sharply. At the same time, the priest started to read, his tone mocking the trapped children, his face an ugly, exaggerated sneer, giving me a look as if asking me "What are you going to do about it?" I thought I heard him chant "Ailsa! Ailsa! Ailsa!" and I grabbed her hand and tugged. We got up and quickly walked down the aisle to the sound of everyone stifling laughs at our expense. I could not seem to open the door, and the sound was like cannon balls being dropped from the ceiling to the floor. But I eventually pulled it open and we were out on the stairs.

"Adam, you're all right, it's just the acid, everything's okay. Fuck that place anyway. Come on, let's go and have a picnic in the Pentlands, d'you want to?"

"Woooooooooow!" I said, "Stumbling stone statues to stay away from!" and I started laughing hysterically.

"Come on!" she laughed, "Packing Pentland picnic Pinocchio!"

To which we both laughed harder and walked to the flat.

Ailsa went upstairs to raid the kitchen and I sat cross-legged on the floor and stared at "The Red Studio," pulling hard on a cigarette. The painting was as vivid as fire, as Ailsa's hair, but dotted with these oases of calm, the pictures on the red studio wall. A bird? A reclining figure? A huge angel against the wall, forever immortalized on canvas? I couldn't tell, but slowly I started to get it, he had painted ambiguity into the pictures on his wall! And just for this reason I could sit and the shapes would change, bird to a prisoner, reclining nude to collapsed horse, over and over again, the flowers sprouting from a vase in the foreground at once benign and menacing, petalled tentacles, Venus flytraps that could read nursery rhymes. The room and my feeling were enhanced by the heavy aroma of the roses, sickly, like dirty angel wings.

Ailsa came back down. She looked like she was gliding, the scent of the roses intensified, her face pure and shocking, cars crashing slowly in a flower bed, over and over.

"Two bottles of plonk, bread, brie, Swiss Army knife, oranges, and we'll get some ciggies on the way. All right, darling?" She smiled. "Oh! Picnic blanket!" she said, and pulled the tapestry off the sofa. "We need a picnic blanket."

"Isn't that a family antique or something?" I asked vaguely.

"Got it at Habitat for five quid, I think," she laughed.

"But it's so beautiful, it's the sun!"

"Good, then we're guaranteed it won't rain, aren't we?"

She put everything into a huge canvas hold-all and gave it to me. "Hope you don't mind lugging it, I really can't be arsed," and we left, walking down Shandwick Place and stopping at a newsagent's in Haymarket where she bought sixty John Player Special, a lighter, and a packet of Rizlas. I immediately felt paranoid that the Rizlas would alert the stone-faced man behind the counter that we were drug addicts, already high on a Sunday morning. Not only that, but I was a sexual deviant who stalked invisible women and dressed in their clothes in public. However, one look at Ailsa calmed me down, she had a knack of appearing that she cared not a jot what anyone thought of her or her actions, a charismatic demeanour that deflected any argument. That, and she was disarmingly beautiful.

We walked peacefully along Morrison Street to Tollcross, the skies were so high, the clouds playing chasey with the gulls, their faces turning from skulls to clowns to skulls to clowns. The street still bore some of last night's hard legend, broken glass, vomit, discarded, half-eaten baked potatoes, giving counterpoint shame and violence to the majesty of the sky.

We were tripping hard. A few choice words and phrases left Ailsa's mouth, but on the whole we walked in silence, hand in hand, as our minds whirled with the actions of everything, smoking constantly, Ailsa swigging thirstily from a carton of orange juice she had possibly stolen from the newsagent's shop.

"We are going to the end of the city, angel, the very end, it could be the end of everything, you know, the very border of poetry. I can't wait to see it, poetry is so close to purity, isn't it?"

"Poetry is purity."

"That's right."

We caught a number 11 on Earl Grey Street and raced upstairs to see if the front two seats were free. They were, and we sat down, giggling ecstatically as we lit more cigarettes. There were a couple of other people on top, hiding from us behind Sunday Posts or Sunday Mirrors. We enjoyed the ride, whizzing by the Links, Bruntsfield, taking in the snapshots of the Firth of Forth and Fife down the steep side streets.

"We're going to pass where I worked," I said.

"Those fuckers! I'm so glad you're not there anymore."

As we passed Safeway, Ailsa made "V" signs with both her hands and shouted, "Catch us if you can, you fucking arseholes!" before collapsing into giggles.

"Ailsa! Don't!" I laughed, but no one upstairs seemed to care, or they were too frightened.

We got off the bus at the terminus, right where Edinburgh ends and the Pentlands begin, and started walking up the road to the artificial ski slope, which was visible year round to all of Edinburgh as a huge grey scar on the side of a hill. I told Ailsa about coming here with my friends to pick psilocybin during the mellow autumn weekends of my senior school years.

The green of the hill was undulating in slow motion before our eyes, like some god shaking a blanket. I was immediately reminded of a poem I had studied in school by an Edinburgh poet called Stanley Roger Green: "Bavelaw in Winter," in which the author imagined on a walk that the he was back in the Bronze Age. I wished it was the Bronze Age, but perhaps it was.

"Come on," shouted Ailsa, "Let's run!" and off she took, me in dogged pursuit, weighed down by the canvas hold-all I had on my shoulder. We ran past the barn-like building that housed the café and ski rental depot. There was complete silence apart from Ailsa's voice, shimmering lightly in the air. "It's like running on cotton wool!" she cried. "No, no, wait, it's like running on birthday cake!" She started laughing again and we both collapsed on the grass, me after her. We lay looking up at the clouds. "They're moving so fast, aren't they?" she whispered.

"They're trying to tell us something."

"I know, I wonder what though."

Our dialogue sounded like it was from *The Secret Garden* or *The Railway Children* or some other children's fantasy drama. The sky was a moving kaleidoscope of deep, rich blue and brilliant white, the clouds changing from an intricate lattice against infinity, to millions of crucifixes, to one huge white crucifix looming over Edinburgh.

"I can see God's hands flickering!" said Ailsa.

"I can see his playroom," I said. Looking out across Edinburgh to the sea, I could see someone in every single window, waving at us.

"Fuck! Everyone's waving at us!" I exclaimed delightedly.

"They're all jealous, angel, they want to be us," Ailsa purred drowsily.

"Maybe they're shaking their fists, though, I'm not so sure."

"Let's walk a little more and have some wine," Ailsa said, getting up. "Actually, in case you hadn't noticed, there's no one in that city. Look, no one's home, there's not a single car on the streets, just me, you, and that number 11 bus." She brushed grass from her clothes.

"What's that moving silver shiny thing down there then?" I asked, pointing to somewhere south of Morningside.

"It's a ghost, lovey, that's all, come on," she said simply, and we started walking up.

The wind was a playful stream that we danced in, stumbling occasionally as our feet found random rabbit holes and stray stones. The light dimmed and brightened subtly and quickly, changing the shape of our surroundings radically as it did so. It was only the clouds passing the sun, but every time it happened, we were in a completely new and alien landscape for a few seconds. We could see the city and its windows coruscating in the afternoon's eye, and when we eventually threw down our blanket, there was not a soul to be seen or heard. We made love quickly, as an entity; we were combined fully with nature for a split second, we were the hills, and I actually became the Bronze Age landscape that so awed Stanley Roger Green.

"Mmmm, wine," sighed Ailsa, kissing me as she climbed off me. She reached into the hold-all and pulled out a bottle and her Swiss Army knife. "Laaaaambrusco!" she shouted and giggled. As she uncorked it, I busied myself trying to roll a joint, which, in the light of the drugs I had taken, was like trying to complete an algebraic equation.

"Fuckin' hell, mate, you're useless!" Ailsa squealed delightedly. "Here, have a swig of this."

She handed me the wine and lit two cigarettes, passing one to me.

The green of the soft, rolling landscape was changing colour in rhythm with my quick breathing and I forgot completely where we were, it was impossible to tell. Ailsa was looking at me intently, her eyes were huge and all knowing. It gave me a small fright.

"Adam, I know exactly what you're thinking, or rather, of whom you are thinking. Get her out of your life and your mind, so you can be mine totally. I am not going to share, and I don't want you sharing, so can you do that for me? Can you just get rid of her?"

I was petrified and, as far as I could tell, completely at her mercy. The mood was darker, the whole area was darker, because she was controlling it: the light and the colours, all her, the speed at which the clouds volleyed across the sky, her, which ones reached the sun, her, her, her. Something had pulled a thick, dull metal sheet across the sky, obscuring the blue. I was crying, and I could feel the tears on my face. No, it was raining. No, God was crying. No, God was spitting.

"I cannot accept or tolerate her occupying even the tiniest part of your mind, and you know what I am capable of, and you know all the wonderful things I can do for you, and there are so many more, so many more. And I want her BANISHED!"

Many words shouldered each other to get out of my mouth, questions, compromises, protests, but in the end, fear won, as always. And in the end, fear walked shakily out of my mouth to meet its adversary.

"I'll make sure she never enters our lives again, sweetheart, I promise, Ailsa. I can't let anything harm us. You can forget she even existed."

"Darling, it's raining, look at the drops. Let's finish our wine under the blanket," she smiled.

So we sat huddled under the blanket, our hot breath and the smell of damp wool mixed with the acid made me think we were in an endless canvas labyrinth. Every gulp from the wine was fortifying, and I felt a kind of warrior strength infiltrate my bones and muscle. A strong resolve gripped me. Calm now, think of what you can have, calm now.

The rain passed, leaving a claustrophobic mugginess. The day, and Ailsa, had started to vacillate wildly between grace and menace. Jackie kept returning to me like a slap in the face.

We continued our walk, pausing briefly at a cairn to observe the city. It was still raining over Edinburgh, the sea and the sky blending into a pearly void, all the buildings were melting into a grey swamp.

"I can see our house, Adam, look! The steeple on St. Mary's is lashing around like a dinosaur's tail! God must be still cross with you," she laughed.

Trudging on, we eventually were without a view of the city in a green trough between hills in perfect silence. It was in this silence that Jackie's and Ailsa's faces were, for an instant, interchangeable. I started, and then remembered, with difficulty, that I was tripping.

We stopped to eat and drink some more wine. I could not fathom eating, so I drank more wine, probably too much, because the woozy red liquid was at odds with the acid, and my stomach started to hurt.

"I think I'd like to go home soon," I said quietly.

"Are you all right?"

"It's the acid, it's strong."

She gave a high-pitched laugh. "Try to ignore the claws at the back of your neck!" she said with mock relish.

"Oh, god," I groaned.

"You know, by taking acid, you're basically poisoning yourself—just a little too much and you'll end up raving away in the Royal Ed. Believe me, I have known a few who have," she gloated.

"Oh, don't say that, Ailsa."

"Don't worry, sweetie, I'm sure the hills will roll in and smother you to death before that ever happens." She laughed again.

The darkening hills around us did indeed look like huge slumbering beasts. No longer green, they were a slate grey, trumping the grey of the skies. We got up and started to walk back.

"Remember that story about the guy on the Morton Hall golf course? I think it was that one. Anyway, this mad woman escaped from a psychiatric ward somewhere—probably the Royal Ed—and she attacked him. I can't remember if she cut his cock off or she crushed his balls with a pair of pliers. Maybe she did both. That story's up there with that one about the severed head on a camping trip story. Have you seen my Swiss Army knife?" She giggled, and I knew she was just messing with me. I laughed too. "But Adam, you don't know, you really don't. I could be a total nutcase with ten times my own strength."

"Yeah, so could I."

"No, you adore me, you'd never do anything to me, you'll do anything I want."

"Perhaps."

We reached another viewpoint. It was beginning to darken, mainly because of the clouds and rain over the city.

"Sundays are depressing, bath and school the next morning," I said for no real reason.

"Well, we'll go home and smoke joints and fuck and drink wine. We'll listen to a bit of music, if you like."

"That'd be perfect."

The ski run lights were blazing away and we began our descent to the bus stop, all of the menace being gently sucked out from my veins like poison, replaced with a still relief as more and more lights became visible. There was a faint hiss of distant traffic which brought me back to the present.

The bus ride home was silent as we looked out of the window. I flinched as we passed the end of Jackie's street. She was going to be leaving my life. It was sad, scary, and incredible.

12 · UNION CANAL BLUES

The boy had left the house unnoticed as his father and mother screamed at each other. He escaped into the silence of an overcast summer Monday afternoon. The fight had been an island of violence in a series of long, tense silences. His mother mostly in bed. With a headache, she had said. For days on end. Tense silence atop the backdrop of the throbbing headache. She said. No noise. She said. No noise. Play quietly in your room. I don't know. She said. Make a jigsaw puzzle. She said. Draw a picture. Dad is in and out. More out.

The boy walked downhill because it was easier to do so. Downhill inevitably led to the canal. The summer holidays were dragging on relentlessly. Every day he had to invent new ways of leaving the house. If he had money, he'd get on a bus, any bus, whichever bus came first.

The canal stretched on. A fat grey line dividing the city perfectly, as if someone had taken a soft 4B pencil and a ruler and quickly drawn a score-line across Edinburgh.

Walk. Afternoon silence. Walk. Faint electrical buzz of nearby transfer stations and telegraph poles.

He saw the boys in the distance. Three of them hunched and laughing over something by the side of the canal. He walked on looking. Curious, then frightened. They were bigger than he was and there was no one else around. He stood behind a bush to keep watching until they might leave. Silence punctuated by whoops and laughs.

Eventually, they left and walked on laughing and whooping. Pushing each other playfully towards the water. The canal.

He walked slowly towards where the boys had been. A wide slab of stone. A discarded bottle of cigarette lighter fluid and a discarded empty box of household matches. Small, shapeless charred lumps, about an inch to an inch and a half. Smell of strange, meaty chemicals. Five small lumps. Meat lumps. Dead frogs. Black, dry as charcoal.

12 B ▪ PLASTIC LETTERS

As soon as she heard the large key entering the side door lock, rattling a little, then opening with the usual emphatic 'click,' she started to put the things she'd taken out back into the drawer with a panicked haste: notebooks, notes, some on coloured paper written in coloured pen, postcards: Rome, Malta, The Canaries. A couple of reproductions: a Matisse, a Klee.

Voices came up from the stairs: a girl's—her sister's—and a boy's lower, non-committal responses. Awkward.

The girl in the room shut the drawer quietly and crossed the floor to a cupboard; she opened it and quickly slipped inside. At the same time, the bedroom door opened.

The girl had on a school uniform, as did the boy, but of a different colour, from a different school.

The girl's is green.

The boy's is maroon.

"You can take your blazer and tie off if you want, and your shirt too. Don't worry, no one's home, nobody cares anyway."

There were posters on the wall: a huge poster for Blondie's "Plastic Letters," and another one for the first Boomtown Rats album.

An orange carpet and a huge shelving unit housing a record player and speakers, many books, and further up, a few dolls and other remnants of childhood.

The boy took off his blazer, shirt, and tie whilst the girl took a record out of its cover and carefully placed the needle on the groove. The anticipatory introduction to Elvis Costello's "Welcome to the Working Week" spilled slowly from the speakers as the girl turned and pushed the boy playfully onto the bed.

They rolled around awkwardly as the girl struggled to take her shirt and tie off.

All the while, the girl in the cupboard stared impassively at the scene through a slim crack in the doorway.

Clipped words, half phrases and subdued, guttural sounds came from the bed. Smacking, drooling noises of messy kissing went on for a while until they just petered out.

"Do you fancy a coffee?"

"Yeah, all right."

"Let's go down to the kitchen."

And they got up from the bed, put their shirts back on, and left the room.

After a minute, the girl crept out of the cupboard, her red hair catching the late afternoon sun.

She left the room and went into her parents' bedroom next door. Distant sounds from the kitchen downstairs, rattling and conversation.

She sat at her mother's commode and stared into the mirror.

She picked up a bright red lipstick and applied it a little carelessly, leaving smudges of scarlet around her lip line.

Mascara. Eyeliner.

Too much. Her eyelids deep black against bright white skin under vivid red hair.

She got up and reached under her skirt, carefully pulling off her panties, and then left the room, the panties balled up in her hand.

She walked slowly downstairs, where, in the living room, she could see the boy sitting by himself on the sofa. Sounds came from the kitchen.

"D'you want a biscuit? It's only digestives, I'm afraid."

"Yeah, all right."

The redhead stared at the boy from the living room doorway.

He didn't see her.

She walked quickly into the room and stood in front of him.

"I'll do more, much more than her for you," she whispered loudly as she threw the balled-up panties into his lap and left the room. She walked quickly to the front door, opened it, and left the house.

13 ▪ CLIMATE OF HUNTER

We arrived back at Ailsa's flat in a wavy, undulating tranquillity. The LSD was subsiding softly, leaving in its wake a lapping calmness that had swept home on the bus with us. Once inside, we wordlessly closed the shutters and she switched on her bedside lamp, covering it with a swath of orange material. The room had a soft eternal warmth in it that permeated everything. She put a record on the stereo, some blissful quartet from somewhere, and we made love quietly, after which I fell into a deep sleep.

I woke up in the middle of the night, I suspect, I had no way of knowing. There were no timepieces or indicators; as usual, the shutters blacked out the black, and all was silent. Ailsa was peaceful beside me. I sat up and made a decision. Just like that. The most important decision of my life, and one that I knew would secure my future.

I got up and tiptoed to the bathroom, looking in the mirror as I brushed my teeth, I realized that the LSD was still having an effect on me, KAZAM!! It was still having quite an effect on me, my reflection was not quite two or three dimensional, something else entirely, new dimensional, my lips bowing up and down and up and down, moving without talking! And all around me the millions of frosted glass whispers going, "Adam, Adam, Adam, shhhhhhhhhh, Adam," with the occasional invisible chuckle. I tensed up, I was utterly alone at this point, I realized, I felt like I was on a stage in front of an expectant audience of ghosts, waiting for me gleefully, and with baited breath, to make that fatal mistake.

I dressed slowly and carefully and sat on the floor beside the bed to look at her for a while. Ailsa the child, her hands tucked under her face, a lock of sharp, sweet red hair spilling over her dark eyes. What a gift I was going to give her, the gift of always, the gift of a life, the gift that would set us free. My mind bypassed the event, the event was going to happen, the event was not going to happen, I made it into an abstract thought, and that made it easier to carry with me. I bypassed the event again in my mind at high velocity and I stopped at our life together. I stopped and saw me waking up here on a bright morning, or perhaps in a little mews house that her parents would buy for us, covered seductively in creeping vines. Long afternoons while she sketched, long evenings of wine and lazy talk, long Saturday afternoons of making love and pausing for baguettes with white wine. Bypass the event, quickly, don't look. I opened her desk drawer and helped myself to a couple of the Armadas – it was going to be a long, rather, timeless night, timeless flight, timeless flight.

I left the flat. It was the dead of night. Every sound I made was horribly amplified in my mind, every sound my shoes, my clothes or I made carried with it an agenda. My stomach was sick with fright as I stared at me in the future. I couldn't bypass the event, my eyes wide, my hands wet with unshed blood. I could feel it as it dripped and disappeared, staining that which is inside, indelibly.

I saw a clock on a spire, an illuminated, pearly disc against the blackness of the stone. It was 12:15, was that 12:15 in the morning? My head was making syrupy, slow ambulance noises aaas everything slooooowed down a little more. 12:15—the numbers were dry sand on my fingers, through my fingers. I didn't know, there was a long time before the event, I didn't know. I didn't know what to do, I had thought it was much later. What was I to do? I could not complete the task, the action, the change! Yes, the change! I had a job to do. I couldn't go back to Ailsa's now, I couldn't wake her. Besides, climbing into bed beside her sleek softness would only weaken my resolve and my strength, the resolve and strength she had given to me, like a gift. Best to keep moving. Take more acid, like these berserker warriors I had read about, who got wasted before charging into battle. I was a warrior now, was I not? I was fighting for my queen.

I took another tab of acid, carefully taking it from under the cellophane of my cigarettes and putting it under my tongue. I continued walking, I wanted to see Ali, he'd be up smoking hash and listening to Wire in his bedroom. We'd have a smoke together, I couldn't tell him about the change, but it wasn't unusual for me to show up at his in the middle of the night tripping, high, or drunk. It would be good to see him one last time, I'd probably not see him again. After the change. A goodbye smoke. I'd see him no more after the change.

It was miles to Oxgangs, but I felt a strange sort of peace between the ghost voices and chuckles, the harsh, glassy instructions and raspy screams. You peel them all apart and there was a kind of airy peace, I could find it in my mind by burrowing through and between all the other sounds. The rhythm of my walking helped me find it.

I walked through Gorgie, past the Gravedigger's Arms and across the Union Canal, my battleground for later. I passed it and walked down Polwarth to Colinton Road and south.

The acid was beginning to surge inside me again. I felt in control. There was nothing but silence, undulating like a huge transparent jellyfish, slow and melancholy. I passed staring houses, the doors making them look like shocked and astounded faces, the curtains making them look like they had their eyes shut. There were a few illuminated windows, and for every light I saw there was a staring man or woman peeping from behind a curtain. What the fuck were they staring at? I quickened my pace. I was almost at Ali's. My heart was pounding faster and it felt like a swinging beam hanging from a crane, banging from one side of my rib cage to the other. DOOF DOOF! DOOF DOOF!

I looked casually to my side as a small, white transit van passed me slowly. There was no other traffic. It drove on and accelerated around a corner. DOOF DOOF! DOOF DOOF!

I didn't like that. Who the fuck is driving around Oxgangs in the middle of the night? Who the fuck is walking around Oxgangs tripping in the middle of the night?

The van again, coming towards me this time, bright lights on. It pulled up to me and stopped, the window rolled down on the driver's side. It was Monkey Wilson and his crony. The crony was behind the wheel, huge grin slashing his glistening face in two. Monkey leaned over, jaw jutting out, making his wet, circular mouth horizontal. A wheezing series of short breaths came out of him, this was his laugh. "Need a lift, ya cunt?" My heart was pumping very fast, a strong, bitter, metallic taste in my mouth.

"My pal lives here, I'm just going to see my pal, I can walk." DOOF DOOF! DOOF DOOF!!!

"Get in, you fucking poof!" I couldn't tell which way to run, my mind now blind with panic and acid, the pale stucco houses of the street I was on had turned into sand dunes of the finest sand, they were all the same. Monkey and the crony's heads swelled up like giant balloons in the open van window, huge, maybe two or three feet around, bulging eyes and gaping mouths connected to tiny bodies. I started to laugh. Why laugh? I was laughing, a high-pitched titter pouring from my mouth, it claimed its rightful place in the air, and I watched it ordering itself as the door opened and Monkey jumped out of his side of the van and came around to where I was. BAM! My head slammed hard against the side of the van. I saw a space rocket collide with the moon and all the sparks and flames turned into angry orange birds. "Fucking joker, aye? Fuckin' funny man, are ye?" he yelled, the voice like a huge drill. He grabbed me by the scruff of the neck and propelled me to the back of the van. He opened the door and gave me a dead leg, lifting his knee and slamming it hard into my thigh. I lost my balance as the pain shot through my leg and he shoved me in the back of the van.

"How's that ginger-nutted cunt?" he asked with mock cheerfulness as he got back into the van. "Hope ye geid her a good yin, 'cus ye won't be shaggin' that again, not a fuckin' chance! And you WILL tell us where she fuckin' bides, and we WILL go around there fur oor tea, is that no right, Corny?"

Corny the crony chuckled, "Aye, we'll get oor tea all right, yer no kidding!" He started driving.

"But first of all, you're gonnae help me and Corny oot, a wee business proposition fur ye. We're gonnae knock off a hoose, and you're gonnae help us, all right?"

My head was ringing like a cathedral bell, my leg was numb. It felt like we were going round and round in the same place and it was dark. There was nothing in the back except some bungee cords and some collapsed cardboard boxes, the acid making the cords writhe like serpents, snaking in and out of the cardboard as the van spun around and around. I lifted my head, hearing myself panting in and out quickly as the panic rose in me. Out of the windscreen I could see the tower block housing of Oxgangs waving from side to side, laughing at me with millions of square black eyes, the orange sodium lights raining sheets of fire onto the van, all the while the drone of the van's engine sounding like my own inner mantra of absolute fear.

I pissed myself.

A burst of warmth as it gushed into my trousers, the heavy wet stain spreading quickly.

Oooooooooooh! Went the engine.

Oooooooooooh my goooooooood!

As my fear joined the engine, I seemed to gather strength, and a feeling rose in me, not unlike a spiky giant rage.

Oooooooooooh! Coming out of my mouth.

"Shut your fucking face!" roared Monkey without turning round.

My mouth flew open and an involuntary stream of abuse came out, it was like uncontrollable vomit just volleying across the van, fear and rage, rage and fear, as the serpents sped across the van floor to me.

"Get these fucking things off me, ya bastard! Not the fucking snakes, not the fucking snakes!"

I grabbed one around the middle and it wasn't a snake any more. It was a bungee cord, and it was around the driver's neck being pulled tight as I bit him hard on his withered little shell of an ear.

Oooooooooooooooooooooh!

Looped sound of a whirlwind of bricks.

It was me shouting.

It was Monkey shouting.

Corny croaking like a frog, hands flailing.

Monkey trying with one hand to guide the van, using the other to punch me.

Couldn't feel his fists, he's the fucking poof.

Blood from the ear.

Taste of wet salt in my mouth.

Thump. Numb thump.

Crack. Stop. Big lunge forward. Hiss.

They were both bent forward. Praying? Silently?

No, I don't think so, not sure.

Oh! Monkey's upside down! Asleep with his legs in the air? Really?

Deep prayer.

No safety belts.

Monkey's head cocked to the side with his legs on the seat, so strange!

Body curled up on the floor under the dash, so strange!

I climbed over the back of his seat, he was groaning, his groans getting louder.

"You fuckin' mental cunt! Aaaaaah, fuuuuck!"

I stood on his legs (I think). I had to.

"Aya, aya, aya no ya cu-hu-hu-hunt," he was sobbing. "Aaaaaaaaaah fuckin' smash your fuckin' skull in ya cu-hu-hu-hunt."

I opened the door and got out, my trousers so heavy from piss I could barely walk, hardly any feeling in my right thigh.

I slammed the door, every sound came back in an elongated mocking version of itself.

A new mantra in my head.

"It's not that you were in a crash—it was the acid."

"It's not that you were in a crash—it was the acid."

"It's not that you were in a crash—it was the acid."

Fucking over and over.

There was no one here, the houses were a way across this black field.

No police mee-maw sirens or ambulances.

Nobody had phones around here, did they?

Nobody cared.

This didn't look like Oxgangs to me, but I couldn't focus enough to recognize anything, just a strange dark whirl.

There goes my heart again

DOOF DOOF

DOOF DOOF

DOOF DOOF

(faster)

AD-DAM

YOU-KILLED

TWO-CUNTS

HA-HA

HA-HA

YOU-HAVE

TO-MAKE

THE-CHANGE

HA-HA

HA-HA

CANAL

CANAL

CANAL

CAN-NAL

I knew deep down in there that I needed to find the canal, the canal made sense. I could see that the van had hit a huge skip filled with rubble. The rubble was writhing! Writhing rubble!

The nothing void had twisting shapes coming out like growths, no, like huge robot men shadows? I started walking into the dark void. I was too scared to go anywhere in the light in case Monkey, Corny, and their little army of snakes came after me.

Loping across the field slowly, grey-black grass underfoot like throbbing insect legs.

Walking under the sea without the sea.

Without the sea.

Ally bally be.

Monkey's face staring up from the ground, sooty and dark, but repeated like some nightmarish linoleum pattern as far as the eye could see.

Sound of an engine, spluttering to life, then dying. Spluttering to life slowly, then dying quickly. Coming back in a mocking version again. Monkey? Ye awake, ya poof?

I reached one of the giant shadow-robots. It was a huge coil of chain-link wire, about eight feet tall. It looked like it had become a tower block for a million spiders, but I stood behind it and watched AS THE FUCKING VAN STARTED TO MOVE!! It was either crawling slowly or whizzing quickly, I couldn't tell, all I could tell was that Monkey's eyes had grown and filled the entire windscreen, giant pig eyes.

The van came to a halt and Monkey tumbled out, the crony comes out of the other side, he's holding his head on. Could I have taken his ugly head off? Shaped like a pink turnip.

No, he was holding a rag on his broken ear. Stupid cunt. Was it a rag? No! Fuck, it's a dead seagull! Where did THAT come from?!

Fuck, FUCK, FUCK MONKEY'S GOT ONE OF THE SNAKES IN HIS HAND AND IT'S WRIGGLING!!

They were both sort of dancing, forward, but dancing.

"Where are you, ya cunt?" roared Monkey. "You fuckin' wait, pal, I'm gonnae cut your COCK off and shove it down that ginger-nutted cunt's throat!"

The words cut through the night like a giant metal bullwhip.

"You fuckin' hear me?!" higher now, raspier.

He picked up something, a broken bottle? And threw it into the void.

I stood hidden. The millions-of-Monkey's faces gloating at me from the ground up, their eyes winking along to the rhythm of my terrified heart.

YOU-YOU-YOU-YOU-YOU-YOU!

My sweat has turned on me, it was my enemy, millions of needles penetrating the surface of my skin, trying to get me to shout out.

Eventually the two of them got back in the van and drove off unsteadily. I could not go back on the streets. Who's to say they wouldn't spend the rest of the night patrolling the streets looking for me? I wished the van would just give in completely.

I continued gingerly across the field, the void away from the van, my eyes accustomed to the darkness, but the acid throwing up all kinds of hallucinatory red herrings to throw me off course.

I couldn't believe my luck when, after reaching the other side, I walked carefully down a small street with only a couple of tiny warehouses and no houses to find myself at the Union Canal. I thought I could work out which way was north, north to where I needed to be to make the change. And also, the van could not access the towpath! Monkey and the crony would have to see me from the street to find me at all, and that wasn't possible, not from any stretch of the canal I could think off until at least a couple of miles north of here, so it was unlikely they would find me.

There was a short iron fence closing off the canal from the street which was easily scaled and I started walking.

I encountered no one. Shadows were seen, figures were perceptible, but probably not there. Anyone out on this dreadful night had some purpose of extremes, just like me. There was no reason to interact, no reason to acknowledge. We were not really there.

I walked in the semi-darkness, hearing occasionally the mumblings of water, the whispers of leaves on trees. I walked down the stretch of the horse and thrown rider, remembering its shock again, remembering the cruelty of our position, the horse's eyes, the rider's awkward recline.

Eventually I reached my destination: the aqueduct, where the canal crossed a seldom-used railway line. One side of the towpath became a steep incline covered in rogue foliage which ended at an iron fence, stopping anyone from tumbling onto the tracks below, maybe about fifty feet below, I couldn't tell. It looked like a bottomless void from where I was at this time of night. But this was where the event was going to take place and so I prepared myself to wait by making a small waiting area for myself.

I removed my shirt, shoes, and trousers, so I was clad only in my boxer shorts. I rolled up my clothes carefully around my shoes and put the bundle under the bush that I was using as shelter from any prying eyes that might visit. I proceeded to make a muddy paste with earth from the ground and water from the canal, smearing it liberally over my legs, torso, arms and face. Then I worked it into my hair, smoothing it back. I got as much of my back as I could, but was not so worried as I would be facing the towpath the entire time, I suspected. No one would notice me from the railway—no one was there, no one would be for hours. I had not bargained on being so cold, but I felt a chill through my entire body that mixed with the absolute dread as I stared. The event, the CHANGE, became more and more focused and irreversible. The physical darkness of the railway was defined only by two angry red stop signs, one on either side, about sixty feet apart that burned fiercely, the angriest of demons, bigger than all of us, forcing the hand of chance.

And now, the wait, the dark, the sense of no time passing, or was it that time was passing so quickly? I had to keep focusing to make it so the drug wouldn't trick me. My ears straining for the sound of the van, could they guess I was here? They'd never see me. Could they be patrolling the West End looking for Ailsa's house? They didn't know where she lived, they had no idea, and the van was ruined. Time. It started to stretch my muscles, down there behind that bush, the ache started as a tiny little knot in my calf and it quickly turned into a screaming awful cramp, I had to stand up quickly and bend it straight. Easy, easy. I stood up, shaking. The shaking got worse when I was at my full height and both my legs gave way. I fell, letting my arms save me. The rustling of the bush went on for ages and I tried to curl back into my hiding-ball shape, but the cramp just came back. I straightened out and lay there for a few minutes, breathing deep breaths in and out. Easy. Easy. Black. Did I fall into a deep sleep? It was a quick black pause, a second or maybe hours.

Ailsa was correct, she had been very clear and I had no reason to doubt her, of all people. It was simple, and she had offered me a life, a magnificent one. She was lying at our home, asleep, peaceful, and in a short while I would be able to wake her and look into her eyes smiling and say, "Welcome to our life!"

The mud was drying slowly on my skin, giving it a contracting sensation. When I moved, bits flaked off, so I had to be careful. The night was beginning to show signs of light, so I must have fallen asleep, random bird sounds jetted back and forth through the dark still air. I could begin to make out most of my surroundings: dirty, unkempt bushes and rubbish strewn down the embankment.

It was quite perfect for hiding in, with a decent view of more or less a hundred metres of tow path either way. I mixed more paste with soil and rubbed it on my boxer shorts, I had to be sure I would blend in with my surroundings; I should be all right as long as any curious dogs on early morning walks didn't come sniffing down the embankment. If I saw any come, I could hide down at the fence. It was unlikely they'd look that far, I hoped.

She always woke up early. I hoped she'd come early, but now that school was over and it was the holidays, who knows? She didn't have to rush to go running in the morning. What if she had gone out last night? She might not come running until nine! There would be skullers out rowing on the canal, children, dogs, everyone!

Curled up by the fence, I fell into a sort of trance. When I was startled out of it, it was because I heard a dog, its collar jangling intermittently, responding to a low male voice muttering, "Come 'ere boy," "All right boy," "Good boy." But neither dog nor owner noticed me curled up by the fence at the bottom of the embankment.

It was bright now, with overcast skies, my pale skin shone through my mottled disguise, and I had to make more paste to cover myself up. While I did this, I went through the plan that I had concocted in my mind again. I had two possibilities, both of which made me shudder with alarm, they were like violent intruders in my head, standing side by side, menacing.

When Jackie ran by, I could grab her from the path and deal a blow to the head, knocking her out, and then manoeuvre her over the fence, letting her fall the fifty feet onto the railway tracks below. I saw Jackie's face in my mind when she had let me in the other morning, soaked to the skin, her care and her fondness. I dug my nails into my palm, forward—look forward, what else? This plan was probably the surer one, because even if there were passers-by, it was unlikely that I'd be seen. This would also buy me some time to put my clothes back on and make my way to the Craiglockhart Pond. I knew there were many large bushes which hung over the water; I would be able to wash the mud off well enough there, without anyone noticing me. Then I'd be on my way back to Ailsa, before she awoke, perhaps.

The other plan was to just jump out from the bush where I hid and push her into the canal, just drown her. The face again, the kind eyes looking up from the water. The pleading. No. Not that way. It might take ages to drown a healthy young person, and it was far more likely that I'd be seen. I ruled this plan out completely as I went through it in my mind.

I searched around and found a thick stick, about an inch and a half wide and about two feet long, discarded by some dog, most likely, and perfect for my purposes. I held it by its base and swung it to the sides and up and down. It sliced the air with a low, sharp hiss.

There was a shrub at the top of the embankment that spilled over slightly onto the towpath, this was the one I had chosen to hide behind. It was dense with large shiny leaves. I got situated and prepared myself. The stick on the ground in front of me. My shirt and shoes rolled up inside my trousers by my side for when I had to make my quick escape.

Someone else walked past, newspaper under the arm and walking at a brisk clip, so close I could have pushed them into the canal from where I sat crouching in the bush. It gave me a fright and a thrill. To be this hidden!

Silence, speckled with occasional rustling sounds and the cawing and chirping of unsettled birds. The almost invisible sound of the still canal, amphibian bubbles lightly popping. The traffic from the nearby Colinton Road barely a light snore.

There she was. Coming from the north towards me, and quickly. Pony tail bobbing lightly from side to side, mouth open, focused, red-faced. Too close! I picked up the stick and vaulted from the shrub. A sharp scream, a sudden jerk of my arm. Pulling the stick back behind me to maximize the strike, the stick flew backwards from my hand and down the embankment, over the fence.

"Adam!" she screamed, as I pushed her violently into the water.

Suddenly, there were more arms, there were arms around me, a roaring voice. "What the fuck are you doing?!" A hot, heavy crack to my face. Bells. Droning. My face in the cool morning mud. Ali in the water, helping Jackie out. Her eyes wide, crying, breathing fast and sobbing. I quickly grabbed the clothing roll from underneath the shrub and took off down the path to the bridge that crosses to Colinton Road.

The event in my mind in a fast, raging loop. Ali and Jackie dressed the same, white t-shirt and shorts. Like two heavenly creatures they were. Where had he come from? Swooping down from the clouds? Fast loop of mud and shrubs. The feeling of the stick being plucked from my hand as I drew it back. The fright as I stood for not even a tenth of a second, wide-eyed and caked in mud, my arm above my head in attack pose. Crude statue of a failed warrior.

I ran quickly past a mother and child, the child in a pram, the mother inhaling sharply as this wide-eyed, mud-caked canal creature came towards her and child, her hand jumping up to her mouth, "Oh my god!"

I reached the bridge and realized that one of my feet was bleeding badly. I dove into a thicket of trees and bushes, dressed and put on my shoes. I was still covered in mud, but I had to keep moving, I had to reach the Craiglockhart Pond, and that involved a stretch of Colinton Road—and plenty of time to be noticed, there was nowhere to hide. The inside of my shoe was wet with blood, it was worse than I thought, and it stung badly. Ali and Jackie were unlikely to come after me, she was badly shaken and probably would not let Ali leave her. They would probably go somewhere or find someone to alert the police.

I could not think of anything more horrifying than running down Colinton Road in full sight. Was this the end? I began to feel more and more panicky, but there was no other way to reach Craiglockhart Pond. I had to do it, and now, before the word was out that there was a mud-caked attacker loose in the area. I braced myself and left my thicket, climbing the stone stairs from the towpath and onto the bridge. The bridge gave access from Colinton Road to the Meggetland Playing Fields, which were deserted right now, thankfully. However, there was a remote possibility that I could pass for a rugby player, perhaps I didn't look so out of place, I thought, as I turned from the bridge onto Colinton Road.

I was now completely exposed. I didn't know if the fact that traffic was still very light was a good or a bad thing. I hurried down the stretch of road with my head down, much relieved when I saw the side street that led to the pond. The quiet, eerie stillness of the small houses in violent contrast to the wheezing, limping, mud-covered figure that limped down the dead street to the gate at the bottom that let you in to the pond and its grounds. The east side of the pond was Craiglockhart Hill, thick with dense foliage and separated from the pond by a path, the space between path and pond also very overgrown with bushes and trees. At the south end of the pond and the path, was Craiglockhart Sports Centre. I was coming from the north end, which split off from the pond to a pleasant forest walk that would take you to Morningside.

Right now I needed to try and clean up, so I limped quickly about halfway down the pond and found a large bush bent over it that would provide adequate shelter. I removed my clothes, and, using the branches to steady myself, lowered myself into the water. It was only about two feet deep, but the cold and the silty bottom alarmed me as my feet sunk into it a few inches. I looked out over the surface of the still pond, only to be met with the accusing stares of multiple swans and cygnets, angry and graceful, patrolling their waters, black menacing eyes boring holes into this intruder, clenched orange beaks ready to snap viciously at my nakedness. Pulling my injured foot from the mud, I kicked it back and forth in the water to try and clean it. The water was filthy, nothing more than a muddy puddle, riddled with weeds and flotsam. I used my t-shirt to wash the mud from my skin, not altogether futile, but a rising panic in me made me scrub hard. Like Lady Macbeth, I could not get clean. I wrung out the shirt and then tried to clean my trousers in the water, eventually giving up and hanging them, with the shirt, on a thick bough. I lowered myself into the water and worked more of the mud from me with my hands. Sirens. Did I hear sirens? I chided myself, of course you heard sirens. Drawing in my breath sharply, I submerged my head, rubbing it madly and vigorously to dislodge as much of the mud as I could. It was a fraught and panicked move, under the water I could hear all sorts of aquatic crescendos and the sound of my fingers on my scalp was amplified to the sound of so many tiny saws, cutting away at my skull.

When I brought my head up, I could hear dogs barking and voices from across the pond. I could see them from where I was; they were entering the gate, two uniformed police and two dogs. I quickly reached up and wound my clothes around the branch on which they hung, so they were no longer visible in any way unless you were in the bush with me, and I pulled my shoes into the water with me. Taking yet another deep breath, I submerged. I strained to hear them under water, but the pounding of my own heart drowned everything out. Now the panic was sweeping through my blood like a virus, reaching every cell; it took every ounce of my strength to fight it back. Between the thunderous heartbeats, a voice in my mind screamed and another was low and measured. I tried to listen to the latter until I realized that I was about to suffocate, whereupon I surfaced as gently as I could, doing my best to breathe slowly, in measured, barely audible breaths, in and out, in and out. I realized much to my relief that the police had veered to the left with their dogs, assuming that I had taken off down the forest walk that would lead me back to Morningside. Jackie had probably told them where I lived. The sound of the dogs and the police started to fade, and again I was alone with the sounds of the water and nature.

I pondered my few options, I could not wait here all day or, for that matter, any time at all. It was freezing and uncomfortable and, like my lair beside the canal, it would not hide me indefinitely, I was in another prime dog walking locale. Time was passing quickly. My clothes were soaking and I had to go home for a change. I did not have my house keys, I did not have anything. All of the streets between Craiglockhart and Morningside were unsafe for me, and in my mind I could see two black uniformed and threatening men standing outside my front door talking to my mother. I had no choice but to remain here.

I decided to climb up Craiglockhart Hill, just enough so that I would be in the thick of the foliage, away from the path. It was dense, and I felt sure that I could hide there for a while; it was unlikely that anyone would find me. If I could remain there for just a few hours, until my clothes were a little more dry and wearable, then I could start to think about making my way back to Ailsa's.

I listened to the silence for a minute, and then pulled myself out of the water. Sitting hidden on the bank, I carefully put my shoes on. The cut on my foot throbbed. I unwound my shirt and trousers from the branch where they were, and then rolled them up under my arm. From a distance, did I look like an early morning runner? All I had to do was cross the path quickly and engulf myself in the hillside, four feet, one quick step. I braced myself and looked up and down the path. No one. I crossed quickly and was soon climbing up the hill. About halfway up, I found a tree whose branches I could reach, upon which I could dry my clothes. I kept my boxers on, and I felt acutely vulnerable, sitting against the tree on the soft brown forest floor. Then the entire morning caught up with me. It looked me dead in the eye and screamed.

I had tried to kill Jackie. I had not killed her but I had made a feeble attempt. I had not thought anything out properly, the whole thing had been bungled terribly by me, and Jackie the innocent had a guardian angel who swooped down and saved her. I had tried to kill Jackie. I had wanted to kill Jackie. Hadn't I? I remembered the stick in my hand, my feeble grip, my circus sideshow grand entrance. They might be sitting down laughing at me right now. Me covered in flaking, dried mud, the fear in my eyes. I had simply been following instructions. Hadn't I?

Ali. I didn't know they knew each other beyond a few scattered social occasions, her party, once or twice after work, not much else. The fucking traitor. Traitor. Traitor. Traitor and now enemy. Tears stung my cheeks, they were angry tears of one who is cornered and of one who has willfully and clumsily broken everything under the sun.

The only thing I could do was get myself back to Ailsa's. No one knew her, no one that I knew knew her. I hadn't mentioned her name to anyone, I hadn't really seen anyone except Jackie the other day, and I hadn't mentioned her name, thank god. No one had a clue where she lived either, our little hidden corner of the world. She wouldn't make me leave the house if I didn't want to, she would protect me, rubbing my head the way she had done when I was so ill. Perhaps we'd leave Edinburgh for good, she'd get money from her parents and we'd go to London or Paris or Amsterdam. It kept nagging me that I had failed what I had promised to do, but that was not deliberate, it was an accident, I was there, I had planned it, I tried to execute the plan, and surely she would forgive this transgression and laud my high intentions. I know I had failed, but there was also no chance of ever crossing Jackie's path again, or Ali's, for that matter.

It was miles to Ailsa's and walking anywhere right now carried with it an incredible risk of being spotted. It was too far to do it by sticking to backstreets and slipping in and out of shops and doorways. It occurred to me to try and make it to Colin's, unless Ali had alerted him, which was doubtful. Colin was probably still fast asleep, and there were other people to alert before they worked their way down my list of friends. Plus, Colin was not on the telephone.

I waited and waited, mercifully undisturbed. I heard distant dogs and owners, I heard an outdoor gym class, birds, forest fauna and my dreadful, dreadful thoughts.

I thought of idiotic Ali, following Jackie like some stupid dogged servant. I went through a list in my mind of people who I would never see or talk to again, Colin included. Nothing added up to the magnitude of Ailsa and our future. Nothing.

14 · CAMOUFLAGE HEART

Finally, my clothes were wearable, but by no means dry. They were crumpled and muddy still, but at least I could put them on and be somewhat comfortable. My foot felt swollen, throbbing and poisoned. It was incredibly painful, so I tried to take off my shoe, only to realize with a sharp pain that it had stuck to the bottom of the shoe. Any movement to try to carefully ease the shoe off resulted in a sharp, stabbing pain up my shin, so I decided to leave well enough alone. This made pulling my trousers on very difficult, but I finally managed, having to rip a six inch tear in the trousers to allow the shoe to pass through.

Colin's was not that far away. I decided to stick to the streets, which were all very quiet. I would avoid the many open spaces, sprawling private grounds, and playing fields in the area unless I had to. I was worried about being spotted right in the middle of a field or garden and becoming surrounded or trapped. All it would take would be for some interfering busybody to report me for trespassing, oblivious to the fact that I was wanted for attempted murder.

Cautiously, I descended the hill, the branches and leaves slapping me playfully as I walked past. Stepping onto the path by the pond, I looked left and right to see if anyone was around. No one nearby, but people were definitely 'around' and I had to be as casual as I could. This was, of course, impeded by my limp. Then I had the idea to pretend, since I was so near the Royal Edinburgh Hospital, that I was an inmate, one of the many who are granted day release. I knew from my own personal experience that any potential encounter on the streets with one of these people would make me studiously bow my head and cross to the other side. This was shameful, but I had no reason to believe that anyone else I encountered would behave differently in that situation. It was one of these things that no one ever really talked about.

If I spotted anyone who looked even vaguely official, I would have to try and hide, or walk past as invisibly as I could. Although the streets were quiet and I was conspicuous, at least I could see people coming from any direction from a long way off, probably before they would see me.

I walked past the pond and up into the forest by the path which only a couple of hours ago had been sniffed and prodded by the police and their dogs, I was a harmless patient of the Royal Ed—just out for a pleasant walk after whatever trauma had befallen me. I smiled inwardly and grimly at my own sick joke.

The path eventually spat me out into a sort of cul-de-sac adjoining an entrance to what I thought may have been the George Watson's playing fields. This area, during the school holidays, was monopolized by old age pensioners and inmates, I reassured myself. Not only did I blend in perfectly, but the police were long gone. Would I really stay in this area? Although, in a parallel life, I am not sure where else I would have gone with no money on me, my mother was probably being questioned right now.

As I walked up the street, I started to mutter and laugh to myself quietly and animatedly, twitching and jerking a little. I was modelling myself on a regular at the supermarket who would come in at lunchtime and sink a bottle or two of Strongbow Cider before sneaking out.

I saw an old man washing his car, a Morris Minor, with slow steady movements, much effort being required as he bent down with his sponge, plunged it into his bucket, and straightened up again to work the soapy water onto the vehicle. He didn't even notice me as I walked past. Turning the corner, I crouched down by a car to look at myself in the mirror. I was quite startled at what I saw. My eyes were pink, almost crimson, burning starkly against a white face streaked with dirt. I was very gaunt and fatigued looking. I pulled up my damp shirt to try and wipe the streaks off my face and it made things worse. I got up and started walking again, head looking down at the ground, stealing quick looks ahead and behind me every so often, trying very hard to keep a reasonable clip, nonchalant but confident. The heavy, sweet smell of all the flora was perverse against the events in my mind, all the recent events. The events could not qualify the beauty of nature, it was as if nature were forgiving me without knowing the depth of my treachery and violence.

The houses all had small, well-kept gardens, abundant in flowers and bushes. Most of them were bordered by symmetrical privet hedges that allowed only a partial view of the garden itself. In one such garden that I passed, an elderly woman, on her knees with her back to me, was busy pruning a bush in a flower bed below her front living room window, oblivious to my passing. Atop the hedge, by the front gate was perched a large straw sunhat. Without missing a beat, I lifted the hat and continued walking. Of course, it was less than perfect, belonging on the head of an old woman rather than myself; however, it hid my face and kept me in shadow.

I was now on Balcarres Street, close to the Morningside Cemetery where I could continue my journey away from the street for a while. The placid day was again violated, this time by the sound of breaking glass, every few seconds a smash. Smash. Smash. Smash. I felt the blood drain out of me as I pictured a mob led by Ali, slowly walking up the street throwing bottles at me, but what it happened to be was an old woman with a shopping trolley filled with bottles and jars, at the bottle bank, depositing, with some force, one bottle at a time, oblivious to me as I dodged into the cemetery. My apprehension slowly thawing with relief, I was now very close to Colin's, and as yet, I had not encountered anyone. The maze of gravestones, mausoleums, and trees made the graveyard an excellent place to become invisible. The place was empty, and should anyone have been there, they couldn't see me. But to be on the safe side, I swiped a bunch of flowers from the nearest grave, the muddy mourner. I held them with both my hands in front of me, head bowed.

I reached the gate and discarded the flowers in a bin quickly as I walked out, crossing the street and into the railway storage yard that took you to Colin's flat on Maxwell Street, a cul-de-sac. I crossed the short railway bridge and was finally at Colin's tenement door. I climbed the stairs. It was dark and silent and I stood outside his door for a minute. Although I was fairly certain that he had not heard anything about this morning, I was afraid to break the long run of being by myself. I had encountered no one yet, and had no interactions. I trusted no one, and I was about to invite someone else into my hell. His face would betray any knowledge when he opened the door. If it did, I would turn around and run as fast as I could down the stairs and into the graveyard, somewhere.

I knocked on the door. The knock echoed and snaked around the stairwell. Silence interrupted by a clicking and low volume buzz of electric current.

KNOCK KNOCK

"Who's there?"

"Adam."

"Adam who?"

Adam well tried to kill my ex-lover!

There was a rustling, a clacking of metal chain and the door opened. I was relieved because he had clearly been awoken by my knock, which meant he knew nothing. "Jesus, Adam!" he said, and stood aside to let me walk in. He was shirtless with pyjama trousers on. I couldn't tell if he was saying "Jesus, Adam" because of the early hour I had appeared at his door, unannounced and uninvited, or because I was filthy with mud and looked like I had been living outside for a while. That and the wearing of a large floppy straw gardening hat.

"Can I have a bath, and borrow a change of clothes and fifty pence for a bus fare to the West End?" I phrased it unlike a question, more like a deadpan statement: beginning, end, this is what I need and can you supply it and then I'll go. He looked at me, inhaled and exhaled slowly, and shook his head. "Eh...I'll turn on the immersion, it'll take about half an hour before the water's warm enough for a bath, I mean, are ye in a hurry, or..."

I interrupted him. "Cold, a cold bath with clean water would be great, okay? Just for a minute, just to get the mud off."

"Aye, all right, no hassle."

"Have you got a bandage or something?"

"I doubt it. What's happened to you?"

"Is it all right if I don't tell you?"

He laughed. "Go ahead and have yer cauld bath, then, ya cunt!"

"Thanks, man."

I went into the bathroom and closed the door, drawing a deep bath of cold water. I sat on the toilet seat and, with great pain, loosened and pulled off the shoe from my injured foot. I took off the rest of my clothes and lowered myself into the bath without putting any pressure on the foot. I wasted no time and started scrubbing at my skin with a nail brush, I carefully washed the injured foot and looked at the cut. It looked like a half moon, about an inch long. It was swollen and deep red, almost purple. I washed my hair last by dunking my head in the water and rubbing it with my fingers. When I got out of the bath, the water was almost pitch black, I'd have to clean the bath. While the water drained, I looked for a bottle of TCP to rub on the wound, but couldn't find one; I would wait until the sanctuary of Ailsa's. On my knees I cleaned the bath with a sponge I found under the sink. When I was satisfied that I had returned it to its former state, I took the only towel I could see and dried myself off.

Poking my head out of the bathroom, I asked if Colin had had any luck finding me some clothes.

"Aye, well here's a shirt and a pair o' breeks my auntie gave me last Christmas, they're fuckin' horrible though man, but they might fit you."

He handed me the items. They couldn't have been any worse: a pair of cheaply made jeans that may have been okay length-wise, but were incredibly wide, wide enough for an elephant's legs. They looked like workman's jeans, but they were clean and dry. The shirt was a long sleeved sweatshirt, black, with an overprint of brown and red sombreros with "Viva España" in jaunty bright letters on the chest.

"I suppose ye could always turn it inside out, ye ken?"

Which is what I did. "You wouldn't have any socks, would you?"

"Man, you are in trouble, aren't you? Let me see."

And he disappeared into his bedroom, reappearing with a pair of white socks. "Where are ye going?"

"Away from here. I mean, Edinburgh. I don't know. I fucked up, a lot, I should leave, and soon."

"I wish I had a taxi fare for ye, man, but, here, come into the sitting room a minute."

We went into the sitting room and he gave me a half empty packet of Embassy Filters and a pair of sunglasses. "I put them on when I'm havin' ma afternoon smoke up, ye ken?"

"Thanks, man, thanks for the fags."

"I'll let ye get dressed, I've got tae hae a slash." And he left the room.

I pulled on the trousers. It was an amazing feeling to have dry clothes on, regardless of the way they looked. I actually had to roll them up at the bottom a little. I pulled on the inside-out sweat shirt and then lit a cigarette. When Colin came out of the bathroom, he brought my shoes with him. "Ye'll need these." I took them and sat down, carefully pulling one sock over my injured foot, which was at least a little cleaner, if not any less painful. When they were both on, I pulled on my shoes. Colin came out from the kitchen.

"I've scraped up about a pound fifty for ye, sorry it couldnae be more, giro's comin the day, I think."

"Thanks again, Colin."

I got up to leave.

"I have to go, could you just throw out my old clothes? They're ruined, and if anyone asks—not that they will—you've not seen me, all right?"

"No problem, I'll see ye man."

And with that, I opened the door and slid out, quickly descending the stairs. Maxwell Street was very short, and I was almost immediately in amongst the shopping throng, people weaving in and out of each other, in and out of shops, green grocers, bakeries, butchers. I slipped into my 'outpatient' character, twitching a little and talking to myself. Hat and sunglasses in place, I may well have been androgynous as I stood at the bus stop which was going to take me off to my freedom. There was a queue of about eight, all waiting to be taken downtown probably. I lit a cigarette and looked up. A female police officer was walking towards the bus stop. I froze, and then dipped my head so that the only thing visible would be the top of my hat. Just another nutcase on day release. Just another nutcase on day release. Just another nutcase on day release. I looked up and she was gone. Had she even been there?

The bus came. I was ecstatic as I paid my fare and jumped upstairs, finding a seat at the very front. It was almost like an observation deck there, you could see everywhere and know your enemy before they saw you.

In some other universe at this very minute, Jackie and Ali were probably talking to the police, maybe at a hospital, or maybe at a police station. I shuddered a little bit when I thought they might be at Torphichen Street Station, which was on the way to Ailsa's. If I were to walk from Tollcross, I would get off at the West End and walk down Shandwick Place. I still didn't feel anywhere near safe. There was a very, very thin film between me and a long fall into a very dark hole. I felt on a brink, in my mind I saw my mother smiling with granite grimness and nodding with her arms folded, "I knew this would happen, just a matter of time, just a matter of time."

The panic was the blind force that pushed me steadily towards my own undoing, towards my own insanity. It always had been, ever since that day in the caravan. Usually I suppose I felt okay, but it didn't take much to jolt it into life like a colossal engine. I heard them in my mind talking to the police.

"He showed up at my house the other morning at dawn, soaking wet."

"He got fired the other day."

I pulled the brim of the hat down lower and stared down into my lap. Upstairs on the bus was quite busy. I had to hang on until Ailsa's, this evening we'd be on a train together, holding hands, and probably heading south. Nothing to worry about, nothing to worry about.

Outside the bus windows, on the street, anyone could be a plainclothes police officer. I couldn't help but look out. At Tollcross, where Lothian Road meets Lauriston Place and Bread Street, it seemed like every single pedestrian was stealing glances at the figure on top of the bus, nodding to each other, "Aye, that's him all right, let's just wait and see where he's going, then we'll nab him!" Every old lady with a shopping basket looked like a burly young man in deep, deep disguise, looking up at me and concealing a victorious grin. Every car on the street was an unmarked cop car, they would, on cue, make a circle around the bus and ask everyone politely to get off, the driver getting up and announcing, "This bus is no longer in service, please step off, thank you." Filing off the bus, shuffling slowly, single file with everyone else. "EXCEPT YOU!" pointed the driver and his cop friends, all of them staring and gloating.

By the time the bus reached the West End, I had all but curled up into a ball in my seat, such were my nerves. I rose and walked down the stairs, all hope of nonchalance out the window as I became convinced that there would be a welcoming committee of constabulary outside Ailsa's.

I walked past the Caledonian Hotel and turned down Shandwick Place. I thought of the shop I was banned from, the store detective putting two and two together and gleefully reporting that I had already caused quite a stir very recently. A pervert with a violent streak.

I don't know if I blended in or not, the ridiculous clothing I wore and the hat along with my limp were almost laughably glaring, but I turned onto Palmerston Place without incident and was very soon at Ailsa's door.

Like a warm, slow rain, the relief spread through me as I knocked on the door. My new life was beginning, it was almost like someone had flicked a switch. I took off the stupid hat and scrunched it between my hands. The door opened and she was there, looking a little out of breath and alarmed.

"Please pardon my appearance," I said with a smile and a mock upper class accent. She said nothing, her mouth open a little, staring at me.

"My other clothes got filthy, I had to borrow these," I said by way of an explanation as to why she looked so alarmed. "Ailsa, we're free, I'm free. I did what you wanted, for us, I'd do anything for you, you know that, and now you can have miracles every day, the miracles you deserve. I pledge you everything, Ailsa."

"Yes, you should... You should come inside, Adam." Something was strange. She looked frightened.

"I know I look horrible, but I'll bathe, and sleep, and I'll be fine, but you need to help me now, because I might be in a bit of trouble. But as long as I am here, no one will know where to find me, it's you and me against the world!" We were standing in her living room, the bed was unmade, and there were clothes scattered on the ground.

"Adam, I think it would be good if we went away for a little while." The jagged edge of panic in her voice was just discernable. Had it been on the news? She didn't even have a radio down here, or a TV, but the kitchen upstairs, perhaps.

"Yes, that would be marvellous! Let's go! You know what I did was for you, right?"

"Yes, Adam, everything's fine. Look, I'd like to leave as soon as possible. Go upstairs and get at least two hundred quid from the office. I'm going to book a couple of seats on the overnight to London, and a taxi as well, and I want to do it now and then I'll pack us a few things. They're upstairs," she said with a quick upward motion of her head, "but they have a friend in. They're in the living room talking. Go on, let's get moving."

"Oh god. Oh do I have to, Ailsa?" Another wall to climb, does it ever end?

"Yes." Her eyes became wide. "Come on, Adam, we'll be in Amsterdam this time tomorrow, think about it. We'll get lost, but we need cash. Come on, you'll be back here in less than a minute."

I paused and looked at her, my idiotic mouth open.

"Adam, just… do it." Her face became the same one that cut me with the knife and called Jackie a cunt in the changing rooms.

I put the sunglasses on the bed.

"Okay. Are you sure they won't see me?"

"I guarantee it. Now go, I need to call the station."

She must have heard the news on the radio, but I was far too afraid to ask about the severity of the story. She seemed very much on edge. It was quite bad, then, I could assume.

I climbed the stairs into the kitchen, quiet, into the lobby, floor polish and flowers. I could hear voices in the living room laughing? Crying? The voices were like a hammer to my chest, my racing heart swelled to sneak down my limbs and fill me. A taste beyond bitter in my mouth, eyes on the ground, lips, throat, throbbing with the heartbeat, it felt like it could lift me off the ground. Bowels hot, long silent breaths. One stair at a time, stone, stone silence, do this one thing, one more flight, a million screaming mouths replacing your skin, focus on your Ailsa through the crippling electric fear. The overnight train, us together looking out into the black void of nocturnal England, her head on my shoulder. Lost on some coast somewhere, the sand in our feet, the grace of scattered islands.

Ailsa Craig!
Ailsa Craig!
Ailsa Craig!
Love under the magnificent stars.

Would it not have been easier for her to come upstairs?
It would take her a minute, and no one would bat an eyelid.
Me doing it just complicated things, did it not?
The overnight to London didn't leave for hours, where would we go until then?

"Daddy!" The panic in the scream, both impossibly high and low pitched at the same time.

"Daddy!" It whipped through the house like a vicious wind. Ailsa is hurt, I about turned and raced down the stairs. The sound of the living room door opening violently.

Frozen actors on a stage, the stage is the lobby, Ailsa with her eyes wide and her mouth open. "I opened the door and he pushed it in, Daddy. It's him, it's him!"

A man, tall with short grey hair, a woman, petite with long dark hair. All of us frozen for a fraction of a second.

"What the bloody hell do you think you're doing?!" shouted the man. I charged down the last flight of stairs and pushed him forcefully out of the way, my eyes on the front door. Turning the handle, I pulled it as hard as I could, and slammed it into him as hard as I could. My instinct pulled me down the garden path to the back of the house.

Don't leave, stay here, hide in the garden. I rushed to the end of the garden and crouched between a large bush and the back wall. The event, unprocessed, reeled around my head like a confused drunk. What had Ailsa done? What had I done except everything she wanted? This treachery, this cold-blooded treachery! She was trying to turn love into stone-cold war and you cannot do that! Not with ME! She was trying to play with me like a little toy! The little cold war toy! Not me! I felt every cell in my body collapse under the weight of grief and frustration, battered by unanswered questions, flattening my heart, spreading through my limbs, my throat felt like it was arching, and then suddenly I heard a distant low roar, increasing rapidly in volume. A helicopter or a plane? A vehicle?

I realized that the sound came from me, it was the sound of my whole body screaming, screaming bloody betrayal. I shook hard with the treachery, the bush shook and I was unable to breathe in. Standing up, I screamed "Ailsa! What did you do to me?" my voice echoing through the void.

After charging across the garden to her door, the last thing I remember was an almost soothing, repetitive thump thump thump, an image of myself lying down on a see-saw in a park, the sun shining, going up and down, up and down. Enjoying the sensation of the thud and the tranquil nowhere of the space before the next.

The police must have pulled me away from the door before I cracked my skull open, Ailsa's door had a huge bloody smear on it, like it had been marked as a plague house. My head felt thick and swollen.

I must have fainted or something, because the next thing I knew, there was a bandage around my crown and my head was screaming in pain. I was filled with a powerful, nasty, black cloud of rage, electric and moving like a swarm of insects. My tongue stuck to the roof of my mouth, and I was sitting at a desk in a small brightly lit room.

Two men in the room, one wearing a uniform, one not. The uniform was talking to the non-uniform.

"He'll be fully *compos mentis* shortly. Doctor said it's a mild concussion, a headache, that's it."

The non-uniform turned to me.

"Are you with us, Adam? Do you know who and where you are?"

15 · ON JACKIE

I went to school with Adam Kelvin, at George Heriot's. I started going there in September of 1979, at age fourteen. I live with my father; I have lived with him since he and my mother divorced. I have very little contact with my mother, and absolutely no contact with Ailsa, my sister. Adam and I went out together for quite a while when we were at school together. I had no idea that Adam had begun to see Ailsa, and to the best of my knowledge, I don't ever remember mentioning to Adam that I had a sister, and neither did my father, with whom he seldom spoke. Ailsa and I are completely estranged. But, it is unlikely to be a coincidence, and I can only assume that Adam found out this information somehow. I did not think that he was in any way obsessed, but events over the last few days certainly indicate otherwise.

We stopped going out, but remained on good terms with each other socially— parties, that sort of thing—and since we lived so close to each other, it was kind of unavoidable that we wouldn't see each other. I saw him at a party I threw after sixth year ended. He came with his friend Ali, and it was after the party that Ali called me and asked me out. I said yes, and we decided not to tell Adam at that time. Ali and Adam worked together, and maybe it would have been awkward, I don't know.

A while after the party, I was out running my usual route one morning, and I saw him. He was clearly lying about where he was going, saying he was going fishing. It didn't occur to me at all that he may have been following me, or spying on me. I kissed him, regrettably, a little harder than I probably should have. It was impulsive and stupid of me, and I had no idea how stupid until he showed up at my house at six in the morning a few days later, soaked to the skin. He must have been outside my house all night, but I took him in and let him shower. My father was home, and he seemed harmless. I gave him some dry clothes, and he told me he had met a girl who was insane and who had cut him with a knife. It looked like something he could have easily done himself, at least that's what I thought at the time.

I told him he should leave because of my dad being around and everything, and I invited him for dinner that night. He left without any fuss, and I didn't see him again until the time he attacked me. I was out running as usual, and I met Alistair—we had arranged to run together the night before. When we got to the

144 • CHRIS CONNELLY

canal, I had overtaken him. He had a stitch, and told me to go on, that he'd catch up with me. Right after that, Adam jumped out at me. He was brandishing this stick, which he dropped almost immediately. He was naked and covered in mud, his eyes were wide and his teeth were bared. He pushed me into the canal, right at the same time Alistair came running up. Adam ran away after a small skirmish. I wasn't hurt, I just got a really, really bad fright.

Alistair helped me out of the canal. I had to sit for a few minutes and wouldn't let him go and get help, I was too frightened. We then walked to a newsagent's on Colinton Road where the employee there called the police for us.

16 · ON AILSA

My name is Ailsa McCann. I live with my mother and stepfather at 21 Palmerston Place. I am eighteen and currently unemployed.

When I met Adam Kelvin, I had no knowledge that his previous girlfriend was my sister Jackie. Jackie and I have been estranged since my parents divorced five years ago. She kept the family name Munro, and I took my stepfather's name, McCann, when my mother remarried in 1980. I believe my mother still sees Jackie on occasion, but she does not see my father. The visits are seldom, and never, ever at our house on Palmerston Place. I have no contact with her, or my father.

I met Adam Kelvin at the Royal Circus bar, and although I found him attractive, I was not keen on starting a relationship with him. But he certainly was, and he became very obsessed very quickly. I made the mistake of giving him my address. He came to visit; my parents were away at the time, they often go away for the weekend to a cottage they have in the countryside. I was alone, and was scared of what he might do if I didn't let him in. He brought drugs with him, LSD and hash, and basically kept on at me to take them with him, which I eventually did. At one point, I persuaded him to go out shopping with me and I ran away from him whilst we were in a department store. He came back to the house and sat outside crying for hours until I eventually let him in, as I felt sorry for him. He was freezing and seemed really unwell. I let him sleep until he felt better.

He then became pushy again, and bullied me into taking LSD with him while we walked up the Pentland Hills. He kept telling me that we'd never leave each other. The drug had a very negative effect on him, and he began raving and yelling, behaving like a wild animal. It was dark and there was no one else about. Eventually, when he calmed down enough, I tried to persuade him to go to his own house, but he kept talking about how his mother had thrown him out, so I let him come back to mine. He must have got up during the night and left. The next thing I knew, my mother had woken me and told me that my sister had been violently attacked when she was out running with her boyfriend, and that the person who had attacked her was her old boyfriend, Adam Kelvin, and that he'd disappeared and the police were looking for him. I didn't tell her that he had been here, or that I even knew him: I was too shocked at the horrible coincidence. Then later, Adam was at my door looking like a madman, wearing weird clothes that looked like he had stolen them. He had an injured foot and a ladies' gardening hat and he was covered in mud and grime. I let him in as my parents were upstairs and I wanted to have him arrested. He told me to pack a suitcase because we were leaving, he also asked if I had any cash. I said no, but that my parents were out, and he could get some from my stepdad's office, he always has some in his desk drawer. When he went up the stairs, I screamed for my stepdad. He ran away, but only as far as the back garden. When the police came, they didn't look there, but quite soon after they left to carry on searching, Adam reappeared and started banging his head on my door. He wouldn't stop, I thought he was going to kill himself, but the police came quickly and took him away.

17 · IT'S BETTER THIS WAY

The first part of my incarceration is in the abstract. Liquid cosh, that was the nickname given to Largactil—it just beat you into submission if you displayed any signs of psychotic disturbance. Now, I can't remember a beginning or an end, I just remember a sort of blind compliance, a feeling of being so tired that I didn't speak or ask questions, I'd either sit watching television in the common room, or I'd walk around the common room, around and around for days, smoking, unable to find rest, but being completely exhausted, it was a giant twilight, interrupted by black spots, like holding your breath and submerging in treacle. Eventually, they changed drugs, I became more lucid, and was able to engage and participate in therapies (along with a few other inmates, I was given the task of putting Christmas cards in boxes with envelopes for a few hours every day, around a table, supervised, while we bickered and insulted each other for being loonies).

I think I have started dreaming again, if that's what you call it; they are really too short and too abstract to mention (lucky for you). They are really just very quick flashes of imagery: the sea cut in the shape of a jigsaw puzzle piece, high speed pale animals running, just a flash of light and they are gone.

At first I thought I was awake because I was not aware that I had slept at all, hallucinating because of fatigue. All this was started by my decision to abstain from the prescribed pills I have been taking since my release. As yet, I am not convinced that I feel better for it, but I also realised with a sort of shock that I really didn't care one way or the other. It was something to do. Quit the pills. No one knows of course. I am quite sure that Mum is too far gone at this point to notice, which is a relief.

When I first moved back in after being released, she pried into everything, and was wholly encouraged to do so by my 'case manager.' I wasn't allowed to drink or go out without a damned good reason (the good reason being to go to my rehabilitative job, answering a phone that seldom rang at the Crosswinds Centre in Tollcross). I would often sneak out at night and buy a couple of cans of Special Brew and go and drink them somewhere I would not be noticed, generally in my room, but this necessitated rising extra early to dispose of the empties (Mum went through the bin in the kitchen several times a day), and this was hard because the alcohol and my pills made me black out for hours.

For so long, sleep had been these great big black squares that thudded down on my night, interrupted only by my waking with a savage thirst, or uncomfortable from sweating.

When I sit up awake for hours at night, I meditate on my window, watching it go from an onyx black rectangle to a pale impassive rectangle of light at the end of my room. Dawn was just another bored sigh from an unknown point in an invisible audience, waiting for the main character to clumsily pace the stage, stumbling on lines, fumbling with props, and forgetting purpose.

It is just Mum and me, of course. When I was inside, they kept alluding to the fact that I may not have accepted that my father was actually dead, that I had perhaps kept him alive in my mind. I suppose they had to think of something; I mean, I knew he was dead because I was the one who found his body!

Christ, the sound of the mealy-mouthed counsellor when he gently probed me about my past, "Do you know your father is dead, Adam?" in that whiny coddling tone. "Do you know your father is dead, Adam?" I mimicked back in my head, yes, I know.

It was me who found him. Me. I had visited him quite a bit that summer. He lived in a desolate caravan in a field near Peebles. I was young, a kid, I didn't know things were awry; he told me he was doing work for a local farmer. This would be the hot summer of 1977. I didn't see him lift a finger. "Yes, they don't need me today," he would mumble. The ratio of empty bottles to actual food, I didn't even notice, his distance and his silence, his tacit encouragement of me to get out. "Healthy exercise," he would say absently and indicate the door.

They made me talk about the whole thing in 'therapy,' two earnest social workers taking notes. The closeness of the afternoon, the walk from the bus stop, the green eastern Scottish double-decker, the winding hilly road to nearby the field, great bushes with dancing ladies hanging from them, partially obscuring the sides of the road, the incredible amount of angrily working bees, maybe due to the threat of rain, the low sky pregnant with water, the caravan sinister and stark on its own against the sky. In any other situation, this may have looked like a picturesque and happy holiday destination, but here it was a challenge, a threat. Dad was a broken monster, he had been sucked dry: an affair with a co-worker, divorce, the affair ending in a boozy terminus. I did not particularly look forward to these visits, nor did he. Mum couldn't bear to hear his name, so there was some strange archaic 'obligation' to send the child over for viewing. This would change in a few seconds.

"Dad, it's me," and I pulled open the flimsy caravan door.

"Dad, it's me," and it was like lacquered cardboard, shaking and shuddering when pulled open with any force.

"Dad, it's me," and I climbed the step and put down my small Adidas bag, containing pyjamas, socks, a t-shirt, James Herbert's *The Fog*, a torch, and my tranny.

"Dad, it's me." The usual odours of old food, cigarettes and booze, but this time mixed with an added sulphuric/metallic smell. Like burning oil? Like a car?

"Dad, it's me." The body is on its back next to an upturned chair, the small kitchenette covered in gooey red slimey lumps and smears, a large burned-looking hole in the door of the small kitchen cabinet.

Without missing a beat I picked up my bag and walked back to the bus stop. Nearby there was a post office/general goods shop. I walked in and the bell rang. I was thirsty and I needed to go to the toilet. I looked at the tired fat old lady behind the counter, wondering if she knew my dad and what had happened.

"Yes, son?" she asked with effort.

"My dad is dead in his caravan up the road and I need the toilet."

Actually, it was really not that hard to tell the story to these two idiotic social workers. Perhaps it was the drugs they gave me that made this kind of solicitation kind of like reading off a grocery list, but I really did not want to talk about why I continued to pretend that he was still alive, and still in the house with me and Mum. Why bother analysing it? I was here in the nuthouse, was I not? Let me be nuts, actually—anything was better than living with Mum alone. So when the questioning started to get too close to that part, I would start shaking and pretend to cry pitifully, bringing another day's work to an end.

Mum is on some kind of pension now. She left her job when I was inside. Maybe she cracked, perhaps she was fired, but her behaviour is very strange now, terrifying at times. Not much sleeping goes on in our house. Sometimes when I am awake at night staring at the window in my room, she'll walk through the flat, uttering a low moan. The first time I heard it, I thought I was hallucinating and it chilled me to the bone with fear, but I am used to it now. She is possibly sleepwalking, but I don't really care too much about it, we exist exclusively of each other most of the time, like domestic pets who loathe each other, but who are forced to exist under the same roof.

Part of my "rehabilitation" is to attend to the house, keep her affairs in order, clean a little, but I don't. Why bother? There really is very little to do. Meals are never prepared, food is rarely eaten, the dust piles up and doesn't bother us. Once every few weeks I will launder some clothes and hang them up outside. The students are still renting the accommodation upstairs. Mum still bangs on the ceiling and plays the radio unbearably loud, but they don't care.

And what am I doing? I am waiting. I was incarcerated and it 'changed' me, not for the worse or better, but it did change me. The events surrounding Jackie's assault painted me in a rather bleak light, especially when you remember about Ailsa's incredible betrayal of me. She wished her sister out of the picture; I took that to mean dead. What else would I have done? Tried to persuade her to leave Edinburgh? The country? She was off to Aberdeen Uni in a few months anyway. Oh, I've been thinking about all of this, a lot, in fact, I have thought about nothing else, and I have drawn a couple of my own conclusions.

And then the whole changing room event. They all showed up as witnesses. After a while I just didn't speak, it sounded absolutely ridiculous in my head before I even offered any kind of excuse. For all intents and purposes, Ailsa was not there, I had snuck in by myself, and was talking to myself whilst wearing a dress and masturbating in a women's changing room, I had to wave the figurative white flag. I shut up.

I got out early, released into the scrupulous care of well-meaners, strict social workers and parole officers who are helping me integrate myself back into society. Strings were pulled, it must be said, strings were pulled. When I was inside, I received very few visitors, which was fine, my face was still sore and red from the entire affair. Mum came once a week, and would look at me across the table in the visitor's lounge with a mask of horror and (I think) pity, talking in her awful 'little girl' voice that made my skin crawl so, occasionally asking me trivialities about my life. "What did ye get for your tea last night, son?" "Dae they wake ye up early?" to which my one-word answers would receive a stone faced nod, nothing more, until, after a particularly long pause she would completely break down and start bawling. "I can't believe ye've done this to yourself, it's a sin, it's a bloody sin." To which I would reply, "Okay, fuck off, Mum, get out, leave me alone," and get up to leave, intolerable. There would be her parting shot as I opened the heavy institutional wood and glass wire fire door, "You've destroyed everyone's lives, Adam, not just yours!"

One day I was interrupted from reading a tattered Sven Hassel book by the head nurse, a burly ex-rugby player who broke his neck too much, but with whom no one would mess.

"Adam, Ailsa McCann's stepfather is here, he would like to speak to you. He's not angry at all, but it's up to you, if you don't want to see him, that's absolutely fine."

I looked up, more astonished that I had been interrupted by one of the bigwigs rather than anything else.

"Okay, that would be fine," I said.

Pretty funny, of all people, next to perhaps Ailsa or even Jackie—who I would not expect to come and see me was Ailsa's stepdad. Did he want an IOU for the eighty quid I took? I was mildly curious, to say the least.

I was led into the visitor's lounge.

"Hello, Adam. I've, um, brought you a few things." Ailsa's stepfather was dressed neatly and expensively, and still had the short grey hair. He stood up and laid his briefcase on a table, opening the snaps—click, click, one after another. He pulled out a carton of John Player Specials, a Melody Maker, and an NME. I stared at him, not knowing where to turn. It was a trick, but why bother?

"Hello, Mr. McCann. Remember, I'm supposed to have broken into your house and assaulted you, and scared the daylights out of Ailsa. I don't know why you're here," I shrugged.

He sighed softly with a smile of tolerance, gesturing slightly with both his hands as he spoke, as if trying to calm a child.

"Well, look, I wonder if you'll hear me out for a minute, Adam. Let's have a sit down." He had a placating tone, and I saw no real reason to not sit down with him.

"Thanks, er, for the fags and the music papers."

"Oh, you're welcome, er, call me Struan, by the way."

I opened the cigarettes and freed one from a pack. The nurse lit it for me, no flames allowed for inmates.

"Ailsa's mother and I have separated. We are waiting to be divorced officially, but she and Ailsa are both out of Palmerston Place now, as of about three or four months ago. They both moved into a flat, and then Ailsa left Edinburgh, I'm not sure where for, perhaps Glasgow, I think. The point is, though, that the whole family is out of my life now, Adam. Did you have any idea that Jackie Munroe was Ailsa's sister?"

I looked at him. "No," I sighed. "Certainly not at the time."

He was sitting on the edge of the uncomfortable 70s easy chair, looking very uneasy. The uneasy chair.

"I believe you. I can talk now, because very soon I'll be divorced and I'll have no more connection to them at all." He paused for a moment and began again, slowly. "I know both Ailsa and her mother are not easy people to deal with at all, and I believe something awful happened before I was in the picture. I don't know why Jackie and Ailsa became so irrefutably estranged, but I do know that Ailsa has displayed a lot of delinquent behaviour over the years, and that she has always coveted what Jackie has had. She had to be warned off her a few times, from following her, stealing things."

He sighed. "I don't think you're blameless in all of this, but I have to say that you have accepted responsibility for the attack on me, and for everything else, and I know that Ailsa just walked away a victim. I'm a solicitor, Adam, and I know people. I personally can't do anything for you, but I'd like to try and speak to some people who might, with your permission, of course. They might listen, and we might be able to speed up your release so we can all get on with our lives." He leaned back into the chair. I liked his voice, it was soothing, educated and compassionate.

"I did anything Ailsa asked of me, that's why I attacked Jackie."

"She's very persuasive."

"She's a brainwasher." I paused."What happened, I mean afterwards?"

"Well, I believe Jackie moved to Aberdeen early, and I think that your friend Alistair, Ali, went with her. I asked Ailsa more detailed questions about what happened, and I knew she was lying."

I looked at the scar that had since faded, but remained on my forearm. "Lying," I repeated.

I had done very well in keeping most thoughts of her at bay, but seeing her stepfather, and remembering the moment, the anger and Ailsa's seemingly frail fear, my heart dipped deeply in my chest and I felt like crying.

"Perhaps I'd like to see Jackie and Ailsa again one day," I said more to myself than to him, "But that won't happen." There was a long silence. "I would like to leave this place. If you can help me, I would appreciate it."

After he left, I did not hear from him again, but I did obtain an early release, so he did live up to his offer. I miss the institution. I made some friends, it was easy to navigate, but, one day they took me aside and told me I was leaving. I'd be released, and they'd help me find a job. I would move back in with my mother.

Upon first moving back in, someone came to talk to me twice a week, check up on me, make sure I was taking my pills, and that I wasn't hovering around Palmerston Place or Newbattle Terrace.

When I stopped taking the pills, my libido came back. I had forgotten all about it, but, oh boy did it come back, and when it did, so did Ailsa—she just fell right in place again, not just in a sexual sense, but all senses, and I started pining for her, the girl who had destroyed my life. I pined so hard for her that I considered taking the prescribed pills again to make her go away, but her pull was as strong as ever. I could bring back her touch and her smell easily, our bodies had been so in tune together and it wasn't going to go away, I knew that, and wherever she was, she knew that too. We were going to work this out, we were going to talk this through, we'd be together again, I would find her.

One weekend I took the train through to Glasgow. I just walked around. I didn't see her, of course, but the absolute thrill of thinking that I could see her made me the happiest I had been for so long. She might not even be in Glasgow, it was speculative, but as long as I didn't know for certain, it was well worth the trip. I took the train back the same day, and the next day I took a bus to the West End and walked to her house in Palmerston Place. I didn't knock on the door, I just stood a little bit down the street and watched for a while, then went back home again.

At night, I had been spending my time drawing pictures of her. I had no photos, and I soon filled up a thick pad of paper with pictures I had drawn, crude, and many of them pornographic as I summoned her spirit to me. I could feel the temperature of her skin on my tingling hands. I took care to hide the pad of paper under my mattress.

My weekend visits to Glasgow increased. I couldn't go during the week, I didn't wish to raise any suspicions, but taking the bus to Waverley Station was fairly innocuous. I wasn't going to hurt anyone.

One Saturday afternoon in Glasgow, I went to a few different clothing shops on and around Buchanan Street, and bought a couple of items of clothing identical to those I knew she had worn. I remembered how thrilling it had felt when I was in the changing room with her, wearing the dress, before the anger. The temptation to sneak into a changing room and relieve myself was strong, but I managed to resist.

When I got home after being in Glasgow, I laid the clothes I had bought on my bed, tights and a dress, not unlike the one she had made me put on, one I knew she owned. I turned off the main light and turned on my reading light, covering it with a t-shirt to dim it even further. In the semi-darkness, it could almost be her! I inhaled sharply, and then quickly folded up the clothes and put them back in the large colourful bag I had brought them home in.

I knew that there was hope. We had a lot of talking to do. But we would put our lives back together again. And soon. But no hurry, no worry, she must think of me often, all the time. She knows what she did, and she knows I have forgiven her, the pull was too strong, we needed each other. You just couldn't do what WE did and walk away. Ours was stronger and so much bigger, and two years, the two years I'd been away, it wasn't very long at all, really.

I did not earn much money, but I looked after Mum's pension and banked it every week, taking out cash for the household expenses and helping myself to whatever I needed (there were savings I could help myself to, just a little at a time): train fares to Glasgow, and money for clothing, Ailsa's clothing. I found a leather jacket exactly like hers, it was quite expensive, but it was beautiful, and it smelled exactly like hers. It almost fit me too, it fit me well enough that I could wear it in my room, thinking of her, and looking at my drawings.

One day, I took out all of the clothes I had bought. I put on the panties and the tights, the dress and the leather jacket. The feeling was incredible. I felt so powerful, like I had control over her. I closed my eyes and inhaled the smell of the leather jacket, it was almost her.

Lying down on the bed with my eyes closed, I just about burst through the panties and the tights and then I came. Hard. Exhaling sharply, once, twice, three times, then feeling an exhausted blush cover my face. I quickly pulled off the clothing. The panties and the tights were ruined. I stuffed everything in the bag and pushed it under my bed. I stood naked in my bedroom, my mouth hanging open, breathing heavily.

The following Saturday, I didn't go through to Glasgow, but went out to buy more tights and panties, maybe another dress, or a skirt, something I could be comfortable in, I also decided to buy a wig and some makeup.

I went to a few shops on Cockburn Street and Miss Selfridge and found everything I needed, except the wig. At Cockburn Street Market I bought a pair of long diamante earrings, costume jewelry that clipped on my lobes easily. At Miss Selfridge, I chose a top and a skirt without asking for any help, and certainly without using the changing rooms. I chose some lipstick and a mascara along with a couple of eye pencils with the help of an assistant who knew exactly what I was doing, but didn't make me feel awkward or uncomfortable.

My spirits were buoyed. It was like a project. I had a purpose, one that was harming no one and would bring me back together with the love of my life, ultimately.

I went to Jenners for a wig; there was a small selection, and I saw exactly what I wanted—shiny, vibrant red—however, the style was incorrect, and it was expensive, but I was prepared for that.

When I got home, I locked my bedroom door behind me and laid out the things on the bed: the skirt, the top and the wig, along with the jacket. Barely breathing, I adjusted the light in the room and put a pillow inside the top. In this light, it was just as if Ailsa was there on my bed, asleep.

I turned on the main light and put the clothes away, leaving out the wig, I fetched a pair of scissors used for cutting material from my mother's sewing chest, and then took a small make up mirror from the bathroom cabinet. My mother was staring at the TV and probably didn't know I was home.

I mounted the mirror on my bedside table, resting it gently against my lamp. It was steady, but it meant that to cut the hair off the wig, I would need to kneel in front of the mirror whilst wearing it. When I did this, and knelt down to see, I realized excitedly that if I were to take off four inches, I could make it look exactly like Ailsa's hair. I could style it with gel and pomade, it would be easy.

Once I had cut it to the correct length, I fetched some Brylcreem I had in the bathroom, and took it into my room. I locked the door, undressed and got the bag of clothes from under the bed. I pulled on the panties, the tights, and then put on the skirt and the top. I applied the makeup, pencilling my eyebrows a light brown, putting on the pale foundation, applying the mascara, and taking excruciating care with the lipstick. It took a full five minutes before I saw Ailsa's mouth pouting back at me. I clipped on the earrings. I was almost there.

I finally put the wig on. I put pomade on my hands and used my fingers to distribute it through the hair, then combed the sides.

I wiped my hands carelessly on the bedspread, and put on the leather jacket, My God, I was Ailsa. I needed breasts, but I was her.

I couldn't believe how I felt. Something else, something far more gratifying had taken over, my nerves rocketing, heart racing, legs almost numb. Tomorrow, I would go to Glasgow and be her.

That night, I gave myself a test drive. I left the house and walked the quiet streets. I couldn't believe that I'd become her, but there I was, walking up Churchill as Ailsa. I dared myself to walk down Newbattle Terrace, to see Jackie's house, which I did, from the other side of the street. No lights were on, perhaps her father had moved.

Jackie had Ailsa's father, and that is what she coveted the most, of course. Little of this had reared its head during the scandal, but then again, the 'scandal' was not about some family involved in a cold, cold war. It was about a naked man covered in mud attacking an innocent female jogger, a man who had been caught in a women's changing room in a department store, wearing a dress with an erection, and so on, and so on.

18 · A WALK ACROSS THE ROOFTOPS

The next day, I went to Glasgow, as Ailsa. It was a Sunday, the train would be fairly quiet, it would be such a thrill to walk her streets—as her! I rose early and got ready in the bathroom. I had run into some problems trying to remove the eye makeup the night before, but this morning, I liked the look, a little more punky with those dark rings around my eyes. While I applied the lipstick, my mother knocked on the bathroom door. My heart jumped a little. "Are you going to be long?" I hesitated for a minute and then replied, "Just getting ready for church, Mum," and carried on. When I was ready, I strained myself to hear where she was; the last thing I needed was her telling my social worker that I was a born-again transvestite. I was fairly sure she had gone back to bed. I opened the door and walked quickly to the front door without looking behind me.

It was a grey Sunday morning, and no one except a few churchgoing pensioners roamed the street. Traffic was light to nonexistent, but I felt a lot more vulnerable. Last night I felt an incredible power and excitement, and now, I still felt the thrill and the novelty of being someone else, but I felt my disguise to be a bit thinner, as if someone was going to point and start shouting for me to be thrown back inside. I stood at the bus stop and remembered it was a Sunday morning, in Edinburgh, and in one of Edinburgh's 'nicer' districts—the worst that would happen is that someone may avert their gaze, that was all.

I got on a number 23, and mumbled my fare to the driver, putting my voice just a little higher than it usually was. I had not experimented with a voice, probably because I was keen on not having to talk to anyone.

Getting off at the top of the Mound, I walked down the Waverly Steps. There were a few tourists, a couple of families taking photographs, and some other strays. I entered the station by the Fruitmarket entrance and crossed the walkway to go to the ticket office when I saw her. She was dressed differently and her hair was in a different style, but it was her. Her hair was a lot shorter, almost like a boy's cut, a short back and sides, but the top was long and it hung over half of her face when she bent down. She was wearing white dungarees under a denim jacket, she had sunglasses perched on her forehead and she was smoking. She had a small backpack slung over her shoulder and she looked like she was looking around for someone. She looked so beautiful, so graceful, like an animal carrying this vulnerable dignity with her. I leaned on the banister and stared. I was shaking slightly. I felt a lump in my throat and I thought I was going to start sobbing because I knew she was not going to stand there for me forever, she would evaporate and be gone any second now. Beauty like that did not wait around for long.

Should I run down the steps to her? She would see herself and me walking towards her calling her name, she would be startled, but then she would see right in front of her face how much I adored and loved her. What was she waiting for? What was I waiting for? It was a Sunday morning in Waverly Station, what were the chances? This was not a mere coincidence. Go. Go to her now, I told myself, and don't run, go with dignity. I walked to the stairs at the end of the walkway which led to the main floor of the station and descended, trying to amass as much casual grace as I possibly could. I walked onto the main floor, a courtyard bordered by snack shops and newsagent's, to witness the main event. The world seemed to have stopped to look at the tall man, handsome and lean, holding her head in his large graceful hands giving her the kiss. Her arms around his waist. The parting as she walks away towards the train, beaming with love and turning to blow kisses as he grins back doing the same with a smiling forlornness.

The black water boiled and surged inside me. I stood there like an idiot with my smudged makeup and gaping mouth, while the world laughed at the comic relief, my legs suddenly too big for what I was wearing, my face like some washed up pantomime actor.

He walked towards me, to the stairs, glancing at me briefly—a little startled perhaps? Seeing such a stupid man? He quickly walked up the stairs, idiot, walking off to somewhere, stupid, ugly, idiot grin all over his face. She was mine, and what the hell did he know of our love? He needed to crawl back to where he was from and never come back. Ailsa and me. That was it.

I was seething as I quickly ran to buy a ticket. There was no queue, and I managed to only squeeze out the word "Glasgow," handing over the money and quickly walking to the platform. I was just in time. Of course, I could not go and talk to her now, I did not want to see her in the sweet glow of telling her lover goodbye until the next time. I would probably be sick, nausea rising in me already. However, I was keen to find out which carriage she was in so that I could follow her home. Naturally, she must not see me, so with my head bowed, I walked from carriage to carriage until I spotted her, facing away from me, sunglasses still perched on her head. She was sitting by herself at a table, a hardback library book in front of her, but I could not tell what it was. I sat down several seats behind her on the other side of the carriage, I stared at the back of her head for the duration of the short journey. She stirred not once from her book.

When we arrived at Queen Street Station, she got up quickly and alighted. I followed her, there were not many people around, so it was easy. What I stupidly did not bargain for was her sudden sprint towards a waiting taxi, almost as if she was trying to lose me.

I stood there, faltering and gape-mouthed as the taxi disappeared. I only had a few pounds on me, and anyway, it was too late, I had wasted time looking incredulously as she disappeared in a puff of smoke. Once again I felt the black, boiling waters of rage course through my veins as I stood there helpless, rooted to the spot. I dug my nails into the palms of my hands until they almost bled. I almost had the beautiful butterfly and she flew away! She had no idea that I was right there with her in the same room. Who the hell was that idiot she was with? Why was he in Edinburgh, and why was she here? Did she come through every weekend and lie with him? In my bed?

Shaking with a rage that would not dissipate, I boarded the next train back. I tried to make myself feel better by telling myself that she would probably be back next Friday, she probably came through every weekend, and at least she was not just an abstract concept anymore, at least she was not someone I thought I had dreamed up all that time ago. I had seen my Ailsa in the flesh.

The week started poorly the next day. I had a visit from a social security officer to find out what steps I was taking to find a job. He was a short man, a 70s relic with a bad suit and a fat folder under his arm. He seemed flustered at first, but when he settled down at the kitchen table, I could tell he knew what he was talking about and I would have a hard time fooling him into believing me about my endless tramping of the streets in search of employment.

"Well, I've actually been going through to Glasgow a wee bit, you know, to look there."

"Uh-huh, right, are you considering relocating there?"

"Well, yes, I'd have to really."

"And have you seen anything interesting? Is it easier through there?"

"Naw, not particularly, I just thought it might be."

"And what about here?"

"Eh, nothing right now."

He wrote a couple of things down.

"Adam, you're going to have to give me some proof. Now, I want you to go to the job centre, and at least have them call up a couple of places and see if we can even get a look-in for an interview, part-time hours would be great as well. Now, I'm going to come back here in two weeks, same time on the Monday, and we'll talk again, unless, that is, you find something in the meantime, then you can have the job centre notify me, I'm Mr. Bathgate, all right?"

"Right, Mr. Bathgate."

"You know, they'll stop your supplementary benefit eventually. I know your circumstances are different, and a wee bit harder, but there are things out there for you if you look."

I saw him out. "Circumstances are different," yes, I was caught in drag in a woman's changing room with an erection, and then I attacked a woman in broad daylight covered in mud. Why not just let me collect my supp-ben and leave me alone? I was not a desirable employee amongst a country of unemployed. Perhaps I should develop some kind of new mental condition so they'd leave me alone, agoraphobia or something. I could always go down to the job centre and talk loudly to myself. Of course, everybody in that place was talking loudly to themselves.

My thoughts naturally turned to Ailsa. In two weeks, we might be out of the country! I would almost certainly have made contact with her. I remembered when she told me she wanted "a miracle every day" and here I was to give it to her. God, I couldn't wait to see her face, couldn't wait to hear about that idiot when she broke the bad news to him! He wasn't even in the same league as me.

I had retired Adam Kelvin for the meantime. Right now, I was Ailsa. By becoming Ailsa, I was more intuitive about what she might do, about where she might be. I knew not to conduct myself like a bumbling man, but to walk slowly and carry myself with dignity, that's what she would do. I wanted to find out exactly where that man lived and worked, so much for jobhunting. I had found a very stylish handbag of my mother's from the early '60s or late '50s perhaps, and had decided to use it. Along with my skirt, black tights and black leather jacket, I was a killer queen. It was also useful to keep money, cigarettes and a small but very thick and sharp fishing knife that had belonged to my father. It was insurance. I wasn't going to hurt anyone. The streets can be hard for a girl on her own.

I was now a relentless and powerful detective, I was going to find that man and work out a way to fuck up his life enough so that prying Ailsa from his needy little paws would be child's play.

I spent the next few days wandering around the City Centre, seeing if he perhaps worked at a bank, an insurance company or a solicitor's office in the city. I had thought about the possibility that he worked on the outskirts of the city. God, he might not even work in Edinburgh, but the thought of riding out the outskirts of the city was daunting. I would start in the centre and work outwards. Besides, he just looked the type, and I didn't want to be a solitary man in drag, walking the streets of some stark Edinburgh suburb. I wanted to stick to where it was busy: George Street, Frederick Street, Queen Street, Charlotte Square. I came perilously close to Palmerston Place; I thought about walking by there but tried to stay focused on the job at hand. One afternoon I bought a bra. I took it home and stuffed it with cotton wool which I had bought in a roll from a chemist's shop. It looked good, but it was uncomfortable at first. It was Ailsa, though, and I made myself get used to it.

I got to Waverly Station on Friday, mid-afternoon. I had spent a week looking for the moron, and he was nowhere to be found. It was with such conviction that I believed she would appear that every few minutes I would startle myself with the reasoning that the chances of her abiding by my pure speculation were slim to laughable, but I would simply stifle these thoughts with more conviction.

If she indeed had a job, it was unlikely that she would be here until after six, even if she slipped away early before five. But I had to be prepared for the fact that she may have left after lunch, she may have taken Friday off, who knew?

The station was quite busy. I walked around checking all the entrances and exits, wanting to miss nothing: confused-looking old people staring up at the rapidly changing timetable, groups of backpacking students, people travelling for business, worried parents frozen to the spot. No sign of him. Wherever he was and whatever he did, he was not here right now. I returned to the walkway, occasionally changing positions and viewpoints by moving back and forth.

I looked in the purse I had borrowed from my mother, took out my cigarettes and lit one, mostly for show, to mask the fact that I was feeling for the little knife. Not that I had a sign around my neck saying 'carrying a weapon,' but I felt a little conspicuous. There was a police presence, of course, but they were not looking for me. Not yet anyway.

At about three o'clock, I saw her walking across the main floor from the platforms. Tight black trousers, a long-sleeved, tight-fitting sweater with a dipped neck showing off a pendant, a silk scarf around her neck loosely, and a black bolero hat. She was smoking, and she had a green army shoulder bag and an air of confidence that made her seem a lot taller. Incredible style.

It looked like she was heading to the taxi rank, so I sped down the stairs and followed her. I was ready this time. She got into a taxi, and I jumped into the one behind it. "Follow, please," I asked in as feminine a voice as I could muster.

The driver did a good job in keeping up with his quarry. If a sharp turn was made, or if anything happened suddenly, I had a ten pound note in my palm ready to shove in the driver's hand, and for me to jump out and continue on foot. It turned out that the journey was not long at all, she could have walked it. We drove from the station to the East End and down Leith Street to the roundabout, where we headed down Broughton Street to Bellevue Crescent, a gorgeous arc of Georgian tenements flanking a church.

"Can you wait a minute, please?" I asked in a hushed voice. I was nervous and excited, along with being quite disgusted by her betrayal of me. She walked up to a front door and keyed the lock; it was an entry phone system. She let herself in and the door closed behind her. Number 8. I paid the driver and I stood at the corner watching. I somehow had to work out which flat she was going to. I looked to see if I could see her in any of the windows—not yet.

After about fifteen minutes of walking from one vantage point to another, by the church, by the skinny crescent-shaped piece of common grass that made up one side of the crescent, and from one end to the other, I saw him get out of a red car that I had just seen parking on the crescent, down the street from number 8. He walked quickly to the door and disappeared inside. Clearly she worked or studied in Glasgow during the week and came back to this gorilla at the weekend. Well, we'll soon put a stop to that, won't we?

I was starting to feel conspicuous again, so I walked towards the other end of the street. He was probably fucking her right now, the thief. I felt nauseous and I thought I was going to throw up but I fought it back down. Just a little more time, I'll give him a little more time. I walked to the corner of Broughton Street and entered a little shop situated in a basement, bought some more cigarettes and a can of Coke. It might be a long night, I thought.

I sat on a short flight of stairs near the shop and smoked a cigarette, taking occasional swigs from my Coke. I wondered if I should leave and return later, get out of the area. I was starting to feel like time had ground to a halt, but I could not risk losing them. At least I knew where she was, but I really wanted to see her today. Or rather, for her to see me. I wanted this to be over and behind us, so we could start our life together at last.

They may be in for the night, that was a reasonable assumption. They might make love and then have a cosy little dinner together, listening to music. Our music, probably. Then I suddenly thought of Ailsa's house on Palmerston Place, how you could take a walk across the rooftops for ages without having to come back down to street level, completely undetected! Surely you could do the same thing here, all I had to do was find an open tenement door on this street or the adjoining street, and work out how to gain access to the roof.

All of a sudden he was there, bustling past where I sat on the stairs at high speed: shirt hanging out of his trousers, dishevelled, post-coital grin on his dreadful face—and into the basement shop, only to appear a minute later with a bottle of wine. It had happened very quickly. I imagined rising from my perch on the stairs and pushing him down the short flight to the shop so hard that his thick skull cracked open, sending his brains spilling out over the boxes of fruits and vegetables that were stacked outside. What a brilliant image! He hurried past me again, back to his pathetic little love nest with his cheap red plonk. I aimlessly followed him, watching him disappear into the stair. I went to look at his car, peering inside I saw nothing of any particular note, and I absently tried the door—it opened! Ha! Thanks for the lookout spot! Perfect! He had unwittingly provided me with a very incognito, and rather comfortable spot to wait. If they came out, I could certainly see them before they saw me, and by exiting from the drivers' side, I could easily walk away without their suspecting anything, this being probably the last thing on their minds. I mean, the idiot didn't even lock his car! I lit two cigarettes, one for me and one to burn in the ashtray. I wanted to make sure that they knew they had had a visitor. I opened the glove compartment and looked inside: a few maps, a pressure gauge for the tires, the usual stuff, and then an official looking letter, the kind of buff envelope with a window. It had been opened, and the address in the window was 8 Bellevue Crescent, a Mr. Fergus Turner, third flat left. Bingo! I stuffed it back in the glove compartment and checked myself in the mirror. Nice, I was getting to be a dab hand at applying makeup, and I was sure this whole look would be a turn on for Ailsa, little narcissist that she was. It'd be like looking in a mirror for her, a mirror of her past. She'd love it.

It was time to find an open stairway. I got out of the car and carefully closed the door, double-checking to make sure that I had not locked it by mistake. Walking slowly along the crescent, I saw that most had entry phone systems, certainly the ones flanking number 8. But further along, I found one that had the original latch key system, where you put in a flat key, shaped sort of like a miniature ornate metal carpet beater, that you inserted horizontally into this hole shaped like an upside down letter "T." By pushing the key down like a lever, it operated the lock inside, opening it for you. As a child, I used to open these sorts of doors all the time with my pinky. If you stuck it in the hole palm up, you could (not without some force, mind you) open the door without the key.

I stuck my pinky in gingerly and felt around for the metal piece that needed to be pushed up to open the door. It had been over ten years since I had attempted this and my pinky had done a fair amount of growing. However, I was of slender build and managed to push it up, thus letting myself into the stairwell.

It was amply lit, owing to the customary glass skylight that dominated the ceiling of the tenement block. Every sound bathed in a hushed echo like a church, and everything bathed in the pale ambient light from atop. I carefully walked towards the stairs, looking up to the skylight. The serpentine coil of the stairs gave the impression that you were standing inside a huge, ornate seashell. I had to be on guard, there was a good chance that people would be returning from work at around this time. I needed to give the impression of a pretty little girl lost, looking for a friend's flat. I needed to have the proper giggling apologies to trot out with my hand covering my mouth, to press a doorbell and look surprised when I didn't recognize the person who might answer.

I climbed slowly up to the top floor, and once up there, saw exactly what I was up against. The ceiling to floor was a good two to three feet lower than the other storeys, and there was a trapdoor hatch that granted access to the roof. It did not appear to be locked, but it was definitely well out of my reach. I would need a stepladder, or something else to step on.

I descended the stairs as if I lived in the building and set off to look for a set of stepladders. I thought about just waiting in the car. If they came and got in, great, we could talk right there and then. Although if they were drinking wine, I doubted that this would be the case. If they left and came back, I would be diligent in following them in immediately and walking up the stairs with them. The look on his face would be priceless, that was for sure! However, I really wanted to gain access to the roof and wait there, the absolute seclusion of it was too perfect. No one would see me, no one, and I could relax for a while and wait until a decent time late in the night.

I walked down East London Street and noticed that there was construction work in progress at the school. It was after 5 pm on a Friday, and the workies were long gone, supping pints up Leith Walk, probably. The grounds to the school were open, which probably meant that there was some kind of janitor or night watchman on duty, but I couldn't see anyone. There was a grey caravan, possibly for a watchman, but there were no lights on, and I could see through the window that it was unoccupied, or the person on duty was asleep. The perfect ladder was hidden under a stiff grey tarpaulin painter's sheet. It was about six feet long, if that.

Without even thinking about it, I picked it up and shouldered it, and walked swiftly back to Bellevue Crescent. Doing this required crossing, again, the busy roundabout at the foot of Broughton Street. There was no hiding the fact that there was a woman in a mini skirt and black tights carrying a ladder; I needed to keep telling myself that as long as I thought this was unusual behaviour, it would look unusual. I had to remind myself that I was doing nothing harmful. It was Friday night and people had more interesting things to concern themselves with.

I decided to lean the ladder against the church side wall until later on. No one would notice it, let alone touch it, and before I let myself into the stairwell again, I wanted to be a little more certain that people were settled in for the evening, or settled out, whichever.

I returned to the car and sat in the back seat this time, I could easily lie down if I needed to hide, and I could easily let myself out if I needed to run. I slouched down on the seat so that my head was no higher than the backrest, and I found that I had an excellent view that took in number 8, a safe distance to watch their potential comings and goings.

Eventually, after I had been sitting there for about an hour, they appeared, holding hands and dressed somewhat smartly. Ailsa in a black evening gown and a short black jacket, a small handbag under one arm, her other in his. He was wearing an idiotic looking suit and striped shirt, looking distastefully pleased with himself. They were both alive with smiles and laughter. I lit perhaps my seventh cigarette of the hour and drew on it angrily. I couldn't wait to wipe the smile off his face. I couldn't wait for her to look at him tearfully and say, "I'm sorry darling, I'm so sorry..." as we walked out of the flat together in the middle of the night. I reached into my purse again and felt the blunt violence of the knife.

Where had they been going? Were they going out for dinner? Was she going to have to sit there, face cupped in her soft hands staring at him across a table while he droned on and on and on about THIS uninteresting thing and THAT uninteresting thing? I kept picturing them. In one scenario she gets up from the table and bolts for the restaurant door, pausing to shout, "Oh, shut up! Why don't you just leave me alone!" In another scenario, she comes back from the restaurant toilet to see him kissing a waitress. Fast forward. Dinner is over. Fast forward. He chokes on a fishbone and dies in front of her. She cries but realizes it's for the best. Fast forward. They are walking home, when a drunk driver skids off the road and up onto the pavement, missing Ailsa, but hitting the ugly boyfriend. The shock on his witless face as he is crushed to death! Ailsa weeps at the shock, but realizes it's a good thing as she was never really happy. Better still. Fast forward! She is taking him out to dinner to break the news gently to him that she does not wish to see him anymore, that she needs her own time and space. Fast forward. Fast forward! Fast forward! Now I was just blanking out him altogether, my mind would not let me gaze upon what she was gazing upon. Why would I wish to stare at something so wretchedly ugly and weak? Why?

I was so used to sitting and waiting now. All I had done for years it seemed was sit and wait, it had taught me such incredible extremes of patience, I could sit and wait for hours, days, if need be. After about another hour or so, the light outside had dimmed considerably, the main intersection of streets at the roundabout appeared busy, but the crescent was quiet. I lit two more cigarettes, one for me and one for his car, although I had already done quite a bit of smoke damage during the hours I had been sitting there, and there was an acrid fug permeating the inside of the vehicle. I finished my cigarette, absently extinguishing it on the back seat, and exited the car.

No one had touched the ladder. I picked it up, walked to the tenement door, stuck my pinky in the lock, and opened it. I walked up the stairs again with such confidence and grace until I was at the top, where, without missing a beat, I set up the ladder under the trapdoor hatch. The sounds of televisions and drifting conversations were ghostly as they reached me. I stood and looked up. Easy. And it was—the hatch opened, I climbed silently onto the roof, pulled myself through, and then turned around so that I could dangle my torso back inside to grab the ladder with both hands, and pulled it up onto the roof with me. I closed the hatch and looked around, the huge glass skylight a glowing jewel on the dark roof. It was wonderful to be in such a secret place above the city. I was exhilarated and re-energized.

Around me the shadow figures of chimneys and television aerials formed a strange landscape of statues and spikes against the dark sky. It was hard to see and I regretted not bringing any kind of torch. I knew which way to go, but I also had to carry the ladder. I picked it up and started treading very carefully on the thin valley between gables and slates. There were wires and odd pipes, even the occasional brick, so I had to be very cautious. But I was in no hurry, and eventually I made it to the correct roof. The skylight here was larger and shaped like a glass tent, sectioned off by thin iron strips, a couple of the glass panes were damaged and thin cracks laced them like crystal veins in the light.

Putting the ladder down, I went to the trapdoor. It was locked, I gave it a tug and it moved about a centimetre up, that was it. I took out the fishing knife and jammed it in flat, pulling it up sharply to try and lever the trapdoor. Nothing. I kept working at it and eventually it gave, owing to the years of rust on the padlock chain. I listened to the stairwell, the same very distant sounds of television and conversation babbling away into nothing.

The waiting again. Everything was in place. I would listen at the trapdoor, which I had wedged open about an inch with the handbag. This also allowed me a limited view of the top storey, which didn't do me much good, but I liked having it. I lay down beside the trapdoor and listened. I must have dozed off as I was awoken by the sound of shouting coming from the crescent below along with a faint smell of, rubber, was it? Oil? Vandals ? I stood up to peer over the roof, realizing that I had had one of my legs folded up the entire time I was asleep...

The car is engulfed in flames, plumes of black smoke belching up into the dark night. People have come out of their flats and are standing amazed at a distance. The figure on the roof scrambles to stand, unsteadily, a dishevelled she-male with smudged makeup and filthy torn clothing. The figure cranes to look over to see the source of the noise and the smell. Finally the petrol tank heats to bursting point and there is a loud emphatic explosion, the force and fright of which throws the trembling figure backwards onto the glass skylight. It breaks easily, and the figure falls four storeys to hit the stairwell floor with a sickening crack, blood, and the twisted body is still.

19 · FERGUS AND SHONA

After what seemed like hours of waiting, and questions from the police and the fire department, the couple got into a taxi and checked into a hotel for the night. The police were calling it a coincidence, but Fergus thought otherwise. No, he and his fiancée, Shona Shields, had no enemies, don't be ridiculous!

Shona was studying sociology at Glasgow University and came back most weekends to stay with Fergus. He worked for his father at a building society in the New Town. That weekend had been their anniversary, they had gone to an Italian place on Broughton Street that they liked. They returned to see what was left of his car—a present from his parents—now reduced to an ugly, squat skeleton smouldering on the street. Had he left it open? Possibly, he had done so before, carelessly. Possibly, he hadn't seen Shona for a week, he was excited. Did he smoke? No, never have done. Preliminary examination had revealed several cigarette ends and the melted remains of a disposable Bic lighter, which may have acted as an accelerant should either a cigarette not been have been extinguished properly or had a fire been started maliciously. These answers would be forthcoming and more conclusive in a few days.

The couple were not asked to look at the body. A female had fallen to her death through the skylight of the building. Suicide had not been ruled out, neither had a botched break-in attempt. Police, however, are baffled as to why a young woman, dressed in what may best be described as evening wear, would be doing breaking and entering. A little later on it was revealed that the deceased was, in fact, male.

A few days later, Fergus and Shona were summoned to Gayfield Square. They were told that all of Fergus's neighbours had been spoken to, and did either Mr. Turner or Ms. Sheilds know an Adam Kelvin? They looked at each other, baffled and confused.

No. They had not.

Afterwards they walked to Broughton Street and hailed a taxi which took them to Shona's parents' house in the Grange, where they announced their engagement to a delighted reception.

20 · ON JACKIE AND AILSA

The Chambers Street Museum café was bustling with lunchtime business: old age pensioners and pupils of George Heriot's down the street, mostly. Jackie looked up from where she was seated as her sister walked in quickly, looking flustered. She spotted Jackie and hurried towards the table.

"I'm sorry I'm a bit late, I was at the doctor's," she said, taking a seat.

"It's okay, it's just a few minutes."

"I feel very, um, awkward and strange," said Ailsa, the last word coming out in a forced laugh.

"That makes two of us," said Jackie, without smiling. "What's on your mind, Ailsa?"

Ailsa shifted in her seat, looking down at the table, and then up at her sister, who looked into her face expectantly, eventually her eyebrows raised as if to ask "Well?"

Ailsa put her handbag on the table and sighed a small sigh of exasperation, put the handbag on the ground beside her seat, and then put it back on the table again. She fished around inside and pulled out a packet of Du Mauriers and a lighter, then she put them back in the handbag and zipped it shut with an air of finality. She looked at Jackie dead on.

"I... I really want to have a sister again, Jackie," she said in a small voice.

Jackie watched Ailsa's face and saw the face of the nine-year-old who used to live in the same house as her. It was inconceivable to her that they were blood relatives.

"You heard about Adam," Jackie stated rather than asked.

"Yes."

A long silence followed.

"Why were you at the doctor?" asked Jackie.

"I'm pregnant," Ailsa said quietly.

Jackie's face froze. There was another long pause.

"Is that what you want?" asked Jackie.

"It's what I have, Jackie. It's...all I have."

Behind them at another table, an argument was escalating between schoolboys.

Jackie frowned in annoyance. It was hard to tell if she was annoyed at the schoolboys or at her sister.

"Who's the father?" asked Jackie.

"I don't know, someone who isn't here right now," Ailsa answered a little sharply.

"You know they found a whole book of drawings of you, he was completely obsessed with you."

Ailsa seemed at once deflated and agitated.

"Can't we…" She looked around her desperately as if one of the schoolboys would offer her the correct words. "Can't we…" A tiny gasp of exaggeration.

"Can't we what?" Jackie asked evenly.

"I'm pregnant, I feel like complete crap."

"You treat people like complete crap."

"Not anymore," she whimpered in a childish voice.

There was a pause and Jackie spoke in a conversational tone.

"Did you know he found his father dead in some squalid caravan somewhere in the countryside? I had always assumed his dad was alive, that his parents were divorced like ours, but he was fucking twelve or thirteen and he saw his dad's brains splattered like strawberry jam all over this shitty caravan."

Ailsa leaned onto the table and put her face into her hands. She spoke very slowly and deliberately, her voice muffled a little from speaking through her hands.

"I know what I did. I know what we both did. I did not tell him to hurt you, I just wanted to get away from you or for you to go away. Jackie, the only reason—" she paused, sniffing, and looked up at the empty chair in front of her, her sister exiting the café, and a few twelve-year-old schoolboys looking at her, grinning cruelly.

ACKNOWLEDGEMENTS

Several good friends of mine have been of invaluable assistance to me during this project:

JAMES MACKAY
For his pictorial tutorial of Edinburgh rooftops.

IAIN MCGREGOR
For his insight to the treatment of the mentally ill in Scotland in the early 1980s.

KATHIE COONAGH
For Glaswegian geography and some notes on early 1980s girls' style.

STU WILSON
For extra insight to Edinburgh in the early 1980s, and for letting me use the house he grew up in as a blueprint for this book.

KEVIN MOSER
My editor.

KELLY WRIGHT
Proof reading.

KIMBERLY BLESSING
Facilitator, enabler, editor, and decades of endless support.

ANDY MCGREGOR
Cover design, and my oldest friend.

SHAYNA CONNELLY
Author photo, and my wife.

ABOUT THE AUTHOR

Chris Connelly was born in Edinburgh in 1964 and has spent most of his life writing and playing music in various guises. He has had two books published previously: the first, *Confessions of the Highest Bidder*, of poetry; the second, *Concrete, Bulletproof, Invisible and Fried: My Life as a Revolting Cock*, a memoir . He lives in Chicago with his wife and two children . *Ed Royal* is his first novel.

www.chrisconnelly.com

CPSIA information can be obtained
at www.ICGtesting.com
Printed in the USA
BVHW040445130920
588709BV00001B/42